OCT 1 3 2004

J/J

JEDI QUEST

THE MOMENT OF TRUTH

JEDI QUEST

CHOSEN BY FATE.
DESTINED FOR CONFLICT.

STAR WARS ®

JEDI QUEST

BY JUDE WATSON

THE MOMENT OF TRUTH

SCHOLASTIC INC.

New York   Toronto   London   Auckland   Sydney
Mexico City   New Delhi   Hong Kong   Buenos Aires

www.starwars.com
www.scholastic.com

ISBN 0-439-33923-5

Cover art by Alicia Buelow and David Mattingly.

12 11 10 9 8 7 6 5 4 3 2 1   3 4 5 6 7 8/0

Printed in the U.S.A.
First printing, November 2003

JEDI QUEST

THE MOMENT OF TRUTH

They hadn't spoken for many hours, not since they'd left the Core. Anakin Skywalker kept his eyes on the dashboard indicators, even though they were traveling in hyperspace and the ship was flying on the navcomputer. His Master, Obi-Wan Kenobi, pored over star charts on a datascreen. Every so often he would raise a chart in magnified holo-mode and walk through it, studying the planets more closely.

Anakin usually admired his Master's thoroughness, but today he felt irritated by it. Obi-Wan studied things. He made logical conclusions and plotted strategies. What did he know about leaps in intuition, dreams, risks, compulsions, knowing a step could mean disaster but taking it anyway? What did he know, Anakin thought bitterly, about guilt?

A Jedi Master was dead, and Anakin had seen her die. Master Yaddle had hung above him in a night crowded with stars, held by the Force. She had saved a population by absorbing the destructive power of a bomb with her own body. She had become one with the Force. The great light had sent him crashing to his knees. He'd thought he would never be able to get up again. And he'd known that as soon as he could feel again, as soon as he could think, he would feel responsible for her death.

Before that mission he had experienced a vision that had haunted him. The only thing about it that had been clear was that it involved Master Yaddle. During the mission he had thought he understood what the vision meant. Yet he had kept going forward, kept pushing. He had thought he could change fate at any moment. And because he had thought those things, Yaddle had made a great sacrifice — a sacrifice *he* should have made — and she had died for it.

The Jedi had held a memorial service in the Great Hall of the Temple. Hundreds of Jedi had crowded the hall and the surrounding balconies and levels. The glowlights had been turned out abruptly. Tiny white lights were projected on the ceiling. Then, out of all the thousands of lights, one had gone out. Using the Force to direct them, each Jedi had turned and trained their eyes on that empty space. The memory of Yaddle had pulsed through the room. Anakin had felt the power of every mind and heart focused on one being. The absence of Yaddle grew until it filled the Great Hall.

And it is my fault she is gone.

The blank space had expanded in his mind until it had seemed enormous enough to swallow him. He could not turn away. He could not reveal his emotion to the Jedi who surrounded him. It took all of his discipline, all of his will, to remain with his eyes fixed on the spot. The grief had coiled around his chest like a great serpent, squeezing the air from his lungs.

He couldn't forgive himself for the mistakes he had made. He didn't know how to get to a place where he could forgive himself.

He still carried that feeling. He could not find a way to live with grief comfortably, as Obi-Wan could. Anakin remembered the days immediately following Qui-Gon's death. Anakin knew that Obi-Wan had been deeply affected by his Master's death, yet Obi-Wan had continued on the same steady path. How could he have felt so much, and yet not be changed?

He doesn't feel things as I do.

Was that it? Anakin wondered. Did he feel too much to be a Jedi? He hadn't yet managed to achieve the distance from the Living Force that other Jedi could maintain. How could he learn to shut out his feelings, to close a door against them and keep on going?

Obi-Wan deactivated the maps he was studying and came to stand behind him.

"We are coming up on the Uziel system," Obi-Wan said. "We might run into Vanqor patrols when we come out of hyperspace." He leaned forward. The instrument panel cast a green glow on his frown.

"You look worried, Master," Anakin said.

Obi-Wan straightened. "Not worried. Cautious." He paused. "Well, maybe worried, too. I think the Council should have sent more than one Jedi team on this mission. It's a sign of how thin we are stretched."

Anakin nodded. It was a source of discussion among all the Jedi lately. Requests for peacekeeping missions were increasing, almost too many for the Jedi to handle.

"Our best chance for success is slipping through undetected," Obi-Wan said. "We'll have to rely on your talent for evasive flying."

"I'll do my best," Anakin said.

"You always do," Obi-Wan replied.

His Master's tone was light, but Anakin knew that he meant a great deal more than he'd said. It was one of several ways that his Master was trying to help him. Obi-Wan knew that Yaddle's death haunted Anakin. There had been a time, Anakin reflected, when Obi-Wan's kindness would have made everything better. Now he appreciated it, but it did not make a dent in his own guilt. Obi-Wan wanted to help him, but Anakin did not want his help. Anakin did not know why.

Focus on the mission. It will get you through.

He had been glad when Mace Windu had briefed them on this mission. He had wanted something difficult to lose himself in.

The planet of Typha-Dor had pleaded for the Senate's help. They were the last holdout in the Uziel system against the aggressive invasions of the largest planet in the system, Vanqor.

An army of resistance fighters from the other planets in the system had found refuge on Typha-Dor and formed a coalition force to protect the last free planet. So far Typha-Dor had managed to hold out against Vanqor's colonization efforts. Yet they knew invasion was imminent.

One of the successful tools the Typha-Dor forces had used was a surveillance outpost on a remote moon. The outpost had been able to track the secret movements of the Vanqor fleet. Recently Typha-Dor had learned that Vanqor was targeting the surveillance outpost for attack. The outpost was in a remote area of the moon, hidden by heavy cloud cover. The land was packed with snow and ice for months, which also meant that it was almost impossible to get crews in and out.

Reliable information had come to the Typha-Dors that the Vanqors were close to pinpointing the location. It was imperative the news get through to the crew to abandon the post. There hadn't been word from the crew in several weeks, and the fear was that the comm units were down, or the worst had happened and the post had already been attacked. Anakin and Obi-Wan had been sent to discover what was going on and, if they were still there, to bring the crew back safely.

The ship eased out of hyperspace with barely a shudder. Instantly the surveillance equipment hummed to life.

"Nothing to worry about," Anakin said, setting his next course.

"Yet," Obi-Wan muttered.

Anakin plotted a course that would keep him well away from space lanes. They traveled in watchful silence. The Typha-Dor moon, so obscure it hadn't been named, loomed. It was known by its coordinates — TY44. Anakin saw it on the radar and then received a visual sighting. He could not see the moon itself, only the atmosphere around it. The clouds offered no glimpse of the satellite's surface.

"There it is."

"Radar sighting," Obi-Wan said suddenly. "Looks like a large gunship."

Without slowing his speed, Anakin reversed and dived. If they could get out of radar range, they might not get spotted. The Galan starfighter was small enough that it could be mistaken for space debris until the ship got closer.

"Hasn't noticed us," Obi-Wan said. "I think we dodged this one."

Anakin maintained speed, flying slightly erratically to mimic space debris.

The gunship suddenly changed course.

"He's got us," Obi-Wan said crisply. "Six quad laser cannons, three on each side. Two concussion missile launch tubes. Four . . . no, six turbolaser cannons."

"In other words, we're a little outgunned," Anakin said.

"I suggest evasion as our best course," Obi-Wan agreed dryly.

Laser cannonfire exploded around them.

"Missile on the left!" Obi-Wan shouted.

"I see it!" Anakin streamed up, making a sharp turn to evade the tracking device. The missile hugged their path. At the last second, Anakin veered off, and the missile passed them by a few meters.

"Close," Obi-Wan said. "They're speeding up. We can't outrun them, Anakin."

"Just give me a chance."

"Too risky. Just get us down. We'll land on the Typha-Dor moon."

"But we're far from the outpost," Anakin said.

"We stand a better chance down there." Another missile screamed past. The small ship was tossed by the reverberations of cannonfire. "They'll send a landing ship, but we'll have a head start."

The explosion was close. Anakin gripped the controls and gritted his teeth. His choice would be to keep flying, but he had to obey his Master.

He felt the response of the ship as he changed course. It shuddered, as though it had sustained damage. He glanced at the indicator lights. Nothing blinked at him. There must be superficial damage on the wing. Not a problem for an experienced pilot.

Anakin dipped the ship and dived into the heavy cloud cover below.

CHAPTER TWO

Obi-Wan glanced down at the surface as they dipped lower. He squinted against the glare. The thick clouds didn't diminish the effect. The ground was covered in snow and glaciers, and the light bounced and refracted, making it difficult to see. Anakin skimmed over the terrain, looking for a place to land.

"We'll need to engage the sensors," Anakin said. "No telling how deep that snow is."

Obi-Wan had already turned to the starship sensor array. "I'm getting a solid reading. The ice is meters thick. It will hold the ship." Obi-Wan read out the coordinates. "By the lip of that rock outcropping there. We're far enough away that we won't lead them to the outpost, but it will be a bit of a walk."

Anakin guided the ship to a smooth landing. The

cockpit hatch slid back. At first, the silence was overwhelming. The cold settled into the cockpit slowly. At first, Obi-Wan felt it on the tips of his ears. Then his fingers. Then the back of his neck. Soon every millimeter of exposed skin felt numb.

"Cold," Anakin said.

"That's an understatement," Obi-Wan said, vaulting over the seat toward the supply locker. He grabbed the survival gear and tossed a set to Anakin. Then he pulled out a white tarp. "If we secure this over the ship we might gain some time," he said. "At least they'll find it hard to get a visual sighting."

After donning survival gear and goggles, they spent a few minutes securing the tarp over the ship and strapping it down.

Anakin glanced at the sky. "How long do you think we have?"

"Depends on how good they are at tracking," Obi-Wan said. "And how lucky we are. However much time we have, it has to be enough."

They started out across the frozen landscape. Ice had formed in a thin layer on the ground, making walking treacherous. In their thick-soled boots, the Jedi had traction, but it took concentration to move quickly without sliding over the ice. Obi-Wan felt his leg muscles tense, and he knew they would be tired at the end of this journey. He only hoped that what lay at the end of it was a short rest, at least. There was no telling what they would find at the outpost.

After a few minutes Obi-Wan grew used to the rhythm of their journey and the eerie sound of the wind ruffling the snow on top of the ice, creating a low whistle that dipped in and out of hearing. His mind slipped out of its focus on the mission. He brooded, as he often did these days, on the tall, silent boy at his side.

When he had been Anakin's age, sixteen, the thought of the death of a Jedi Master had been inconceivable. He had been in tight spots with Qui-Gon — his Master had even been captured by a deranged scientist named Jenna Zan Arbor, who had imprisoned him in order to study the Force — but it had never occurred to him that Qui-Gon could be killed. He had assumed that a being so strong in the Force could cheat death.

Now he knew better. He had seen Jedi Masters fall. He still remembered the horror he felt as he saw the life drain from Qui-Gon's eyes on Naboo. Recently the Jedi Order had lost another Master, Yarael Poof.

The galaxy was a rougher, harder place. Lawlessness was growing. Obi-Wan knew now that the Jedi were far from invincible. That knowledge had made him more careful, perhaps a bit less willing to risk too much. Which could be good, and bad, depending. As he settled into his life as a Jedi Master, Obi-Wan was very aware that his need to control situations, to look at all sides of an issue, would conflict with the desires of his head-strong apprentice. He saw conflict ahead but he also saw himself unable to stop his movement toward it.

Anakin was powerful. Anakin was young. These two facts could collide with the power and heat of a fusion furnace.

Obi-Wan had gone over and over in his mind what had happened with Master Yaddle. He could not see any way that he could have prevented it.

His Padawan had relied on his command of the Force and on his absolute conviction that he was taking the only possible path, and events had overtaken him. Obi-Wan had no doubt that Yaddle had seen her own death coming. She had decided it was necessary that she become one with the Force. She had done it to save countless lives, and she must have seen that Anakin's path was mapped out otherwise.

Obi-Wan didn't know how much Anakin blamed himself, but he knew that his apprentice was brooding over what had gone wrong. It was appropriate that he do so, but not appropriate for him to blame himself.

Yet how can I stop him from doing so, if I blame him myself?

Blame was not something a Jedi was supposed to

feel. Obi-Wan knew he was wrong. He tried to look at what had happened in a measured way, but he kept circling back to the fact that in his heart, he believed that Anakin could have somehow prevented Yaddle's death.

He told himself that if Anakin had made mistakes, they came from a place that was pure. It was not in the Jedi code to second-guess another Jedi's decisions. But Obi-Wan knew his words of comfort had a hollow core, and he suspected that Anakin knew it, too.

The distance between them continued to grow. Yaddle's death had changed them both.

No, Obi-Wan corrected himself. *The distance had been growing before that. Perhaps it has always been there. Perhaps I didn't want to see it.*

Anakin's pure connection to the Force meant that in some ways Obi-Wan had little to teach him. At least it seemed that Anakin was beginning to think that. Yet Obi-Wan knew he still had so much to give him. Being a Jedi involved more than commanding the Force — it involved the inner serenity needed to access that Force in the best way. Yaddle's death had shaken Obi-Wan to the core. Was it possible that Anakin had too much power?

Obi-Wan would not give up on Anakin. It was his duty as a Master to teach his apprentice, to help him become a Jedi Knight. All he knew was that he never seemed to have time to address the problem of the tension between them. Every day was packed with things to do, with travel, with missions or Council meetings. The galaxy teemed with trouble. The Senate was sometimes mired in procedures. The problems of an apprentice and his Master got lost in the chaos that surrounded them.

Obi-Wan was all too aware that guilt and shame could percolate and turn into anger, and he was alert for the signs of it. So far, Anakin just seemed remote. This, he had to remind himself, was normal for a young man of sixteen.

That is what you keep telling yourself. But is it true?

His mind had circled around to the beginning. Obi-Wan let out a puff of exasperation, which he hoped Anakin did not hear. He concentrated on his steps through the icy snow.

The kilometers passed in silence. The outpost was tucked into a mountain range that rose from the glaciers. Obi-Wan thought he could make out its outline in the distance with the electrobinoculars, but it was hard to be sure. Land and sky merged in a sea of white. The clouds seemed to lower as they walked, and a few flakes separated from the thick blanket above them and drifted lazily down. Soon the flakes thickened and the wind freshened, driving the snow against their faces.

Obi-Wan looked at the horizon. A silvery clump of

snow seemed to be falling fast against the white sky. But he wasn't seeing snowflakes. It was a cruiser.

"Surveillance," he said crisply to Anakin. "Drop down."

It was the only thing to do. There was no cover. They dropped to the ground, their faces in the snow. From above, their white survival gear would blend with the landscape. They heard the *whirr* of the engines above and stayed perfectly still. The ship was going slowly, tacking over the area in a sweep. Obi-Wan slowed down his breathing and his life processes, a Jedi technique. He knew Anakin would do the same. It would make it difficult for a life-form sensor to pick up their traces. The cold would help them, too.

Obi-Wan didn't think of the cold, or the imminent danger. He let his mind slow as his body processes had. He made himself a blank, just another piece of white against a white background.

The *whirr* of the engines softened and waned. They waited until they could hear nothing, concentrating so hard that Obi-Wan heard the tiny *plink plink* of the icy snowflakes hitting the ground beside him.

Anakin rolled over. Ice had caked in his hair. He blinked the snow off his eyelashes. "I feel like a frozen jujasickle."

"You look like one, too. But it's better than being shot at."

"If you say so." Anakin stood and dusted the snow off his legs.

"They'll be back. We'd better hurry." Obi-Wan consulted the map on his datapad. "We're close. We have to be careful now. We don't want to lead the Vanqors to the outpost."

"Let's hope they don't find the —"

A loud explosion suddenly sounded. Obi-Wan and Anakin turned back the way they had come. Obi-Wan put the electrobinoculars to his eyes. He saw a thin plume of smoke.

"They blew up our ship," he said.

They didn't need to say out loud what they were thinking. If the ship at the outpost wasn't operable, they could be stuck on the moon for some time. If the outpost was destroyed, they would have no shelter.

They found the strength to move faster. There wasn't much daylight left, and traveling in the darkness would be difficult. At least moving faster kept them warmer. The snow continued to fall and then turned into a blizzard. The falling temperature transformed the flakes into icy pellets that stung their cheeks. Despite his discomfort, Obi-Wan was grateful for the storm. It would hamper the search effort by the Vanqors.

"The shortest route will be over the glaciers," he

yelled over the noise of the storm to Anakin. "It's also the hardest."

"Let's do it," Anakin shouted back. They both knew that the sooner they found shelter, the safer they would be.

The glaciers loomed ahead, tall blocks of ice hundreds of meters thick, some rising up to create mountains of ice. They began to climb upward, using their cable launchers to haul themselves directly up the sheer face of the ice. Despite their thermal gloves, their fingers felt frozen. It was hard to grab the cable and find purchase on the ice. Obi-Wan saw the effort and strain on his Padawan's face, and he felt it in his own body as he pushed forward, every meter a battle now.

After several hours of hard climbing, they were close to the coordinates of the outpost. The climbing was more gradual now, and they were able to move faster. The darkness grew around them.

Obi-Wan checked the coordinates. "The outpost should be right here."

He squinted ahead in the now-gloomy light. He saw nothing, just the same blank whiteness that they'd been traveling in since they'd started. Had his eyesight been affected? He checked the coordinates again.

"I know where it is," Anakin said suddenly, striding forward.

Obi-Wan followed him. He relied on coordinates. Anakin relied on his perceptions. He couldn't see it, but he could feel it.

Ahead, what at first appeared to be a sheer ice cliff was really the wall of the outpost. Obi-Wan could now see that ice had completely covered the structure, which was made of a thick white material able to withstand extreme cold without cracking.

There seemed to be no entry, and no way to alert anyone inside that they were there. Anakin pounded on the wall. There was no response.

Now that they were standing still, the wind and cold cut into them, insinuating cold fingers inside their clothes. Obi-Wan wondered if they would have to set up camp and try again in the morning.

Just then the ice began to groan. A door slowly eased open, pushing against the ice that caked it. It stopped halfway.

A slender human woman stood, her hands on a blaster pointed at them.

"We are Jedi, sent by Typha-Dor," Obi-Wan said. "You must be Shalini."

He had studied the text docs of the crew during the

journey from the Temple. Shalini was the crew leader. Her husband, Mezdec, was the communications officer.

Slowly, the blaster lowered. Shalini's silvery eyes sent them a sharp glance. "So our leaders have remembered we exist."

"They could not reach you. Your comm unit is down."

"I'm aware of that. It's been down for over a month. Glad they decided to check on us." She stood aside. "Come in."

Obi-Wan ducked his head to get through the doorway. They stood at the entrance to a small room. The lights were at half power. A weapons rack stood to one side. On the other was a console with surveillance and data equipment. Another console was near the doorway. Obi-Wan noted that it was damaged, with scorch marks indicating close blaster fire. Positioned around the room were four other crew members, all with blasters pointed at the doorway.

"It's all right," Shalini said. "They've been sent by Typha-Dor." She tucked her blaster into her belt.

One man leaned against the wall and closed his eyes. He looked weak and pale. "About time."

A tall, muscular woman slipped her blaster into a shoulder holster. "Past time."

The welcome wasn't quite the friendly one Obi-Wan

had imagined. Then a tall man in a thick pullover strode forward. "Don't mind us. It's been a long haul. We're very glad to see you."

"This is Mezdec," Shalini said. "He's our first officer. I am Shalini, the leader of the group. The others are Thik" — the weak-looking man nodded at them — "Rajana, and Olanz." The muscular woman nodded curtly at them, and the other man, bald and as tall as Mezdec, raised a hand in greeting.

"But where are the rest?" Obi-Wan asked. "There are supposed to be ten of you."

"Not anymore," Shalini said. "We had a saboteur in our midst. Samdew was the communications officer. We discovered that he was a spy for the Vanqors. He destroyed our comm system right after we were able to intercept the Vanqor invasion plans."

"He also disabled our transport," Mezdec said. "So we've been stuck here. We're almost out of food, so we're especially glad to see you."

"In that case, let's begin with a meal." Obi-Wan reached for his survival pack. "We brought extra rations in case."

He and Anakin doled out the protein packs. The group sat down and split up the food. While they ate, Obi-Wan scanned the equipment. He took a second look at the damaged comm control console. "What happened?"

"It was the middle of the night," Mezdec said. He swallowed and pushed the rest of his food away. "I was awake, and I heard Samdew at the comm unit. I thought he was doing a sweep — we monitored the channels constantly, and I assumed he was checking to see if anything turned up. I was awake anyway, so I got up to see if anything was happening."

"There was quite a bit of chatter on the system," Shalini said. "The Vanqors knew we had been able to monitor their comm channels. In order to confuse us, they'd flood us with information. That made Samdew a crucial member of our team. He was our senior information analyst."

"I stood in the doorway. He didn't hear me," Mezdec said, his eyes clouding at the memory. "And I saw that he wasn't monitoring transmissions. He was transmitting *to* the Vanqor fleet. I realized he was a spy. I blasted the console. I didn't know what else to do. It was the fastest way to stop him. I didn't want to kill him. But he turned and moved toward me, and the next shot hit him in the chest."

"It's all right, Mezdec," Shalini said quietly. She put her hand on his arm.

"I heard the blaster fire," Rajana said, taking up the account, as Mezdec had fallen silent. "I heard Samdew fall, and I ran in. While he was on the ground, he tried to shoot Mezdec just as Thik came in after me. Thik was hit in the knee and went down." Rajana looked at Mezdec. "I was the one who fired the fatal blast. Not you."

"Samdew died," Shalini said. "What we didn't know was that before he died, he activated the fire system in the sleeping quarters. The room goes into lockdown, and all the oxygen is sucked out."

"He had disabled the warning siren, but not the procedure. Four of our crew were in there," Mezdec said. "They suffocated. By the time we realized what had happened, they were dead."

"He meant for all of you to be in there," Anakin said.

"Yes," Shalini said. "We imagine that he was sending his last transmission. He didn't need to be under-cover anymore, and the easiest thing to do was get rid of us."

"If the Vanqors know your location, why haven't they attacked?" Obi-Wan asked.

Shalini shook her head. "We don't think they do. We think Samdew was in deep cover. He never sent a transmission before that night, and Mezdec stopped him before the transmission went through. All transmissions were coded and timed, so we would have known if he'd been in contact with the Vanqors. We assume that his mission was to remain until we had cracked the Vanqor code and learned something vital."

"Which we did," Rajana said.

"Yes, let's get back to that," Obi-Wan said. "What have you learned?"

"We have the details of the Vanqor invasion plans," Shalini said. "Troop movements, coordinates, the invasion sites. We have it all on this." Shalini held up a small disk. "It's crucial that we get the information to Typha-Dor."

"We'll have to leave from here," Obi-Wan told her. "We have good reason to believe that the Vanqors have destroyed our ship. I'm afraid it's only a matter of time before they find this outpost."

"Samdew sabotaged the transport," Mezdec reminded them. "I can fix anything, but I can't fix it."

Anakin stood. "Let me try."

CHAPTER THREE

Anakin disappeared into the transport hangar. Obi-Wan had no doubt that if anyone could fix the vehicle, it would be Anakin. He had a genius for fixing the unfixable.

Shalini looked worried. "Mezdec has tried for weeks to fix the ship. With all possible respect for your apprentice, he'll never be able to get it up and running. Are you certain nothing can be salvaged from your transport? Maybe we should chance a walk there. We don't know for sure that Vanqor has set an ambush. There might be parts we could use. I'll go, if you can give me the coordinates."

"Shalini, no," Mezdec protested. "It's too dangerous."

"No, it's not," Shalini said. "It's necessary."

"You'd never make it at night," Mezdec argued. "Survival gear can't protect you from that kind of cold. Besides, you know the rule. We only go in pairs." He touched her hand. "As you and I do," he said in a gentle tone.

She smiled, but shook her head. "We should try every avenue. I am responsible for this disk." She touched her belt, where she had tucked the disk into a hidden slit. "I have another idea. We could return to the Jedi ship, expecting an ambush. A few of us could pretend to surrender. Then the others could attack the Vanqor ship. We could get off-planet in their transport."

"That's a highly unlikely scenario," Obi-Wan said. "And a last resort. Let's give Anakin a chance before we make that decision."

Everyone ignored Obi-Wan. "Maybe we should split the team," Olanz said. "A few of us could go with Shalini at first light. We could take the missile tube and some flechette launchers."

"Our strength is in our numbers," Rajana argued. "We should remain together."

"Thik can't travel," Mezdec pointed out.

"I can travel," Thik said. "Just not very fast."

"And what of the ones who remain behind?" Rajana asked. "We're almost out of heating fuel. Whoever stayed would be facing death."

"We have faced death all along," Thik said.

"That doesn't mean we should invite it in," Mezdec said.

Thik smiled slightly. "Isn't this just like our home-world. We spend so long arguing about what's the best way to do something that we never get anything done."

"That doesn't mean we should be invaded," Rajana said sharply.

Shalini turned to Obi-Wan. "We've been cooped up together for too long," she said. She gave a tense smile. "When we haven't been trying to find a way to get off this moon, we've been arguing about the best way to do it. Thik has a point."

"Typha-Dor is lucky," Thik said. "We are rich in re-sources. We have abundant sunshine and water. Our world is large and varied. We have a large workforce. Yet we have never learned how to truly manage our re-sources and turn them into the wealth we need."

"Yes, yes," Rajana said impatiently. "And Vanqor is a small, dusty planet. Yet they have learned how to get the most out of what they have. Their industries are booming. They are wealthier than us, despite their small size. That does not mean they deserve to con-quer our star system!"

"I am not defending Vanqor's aggression," Thik said. "You know that, Rajana. Why am I here, if not to sacrifice my life if I must for my homeworld? I am just saying that even Vanqor could have lessons to teach us."

"The Vanqors are greedy and ruthless," Mezdec said darkly. "If they have something to teach us, I have no desire to learn it."

"It is that attitude that sets us up for conflict in the first place," Thik said. "If we had been more willing to negotiate years ago, we would not be facing invasion now."

Mezdec stood. "I am beginning to wonder who the traitor is here!" he bellowed.

Shalini put her hand on her husband's arm. "Sit," she said softly.

After a moment's deliberation, Mezdec sat down.

"Would anyone like another protein bar?" Obi-Wan tried. Everyone ignored him again.

The tension was thick in the room. It was no wonder, Obi-Wan thought. They had been together for over a year. They had been hunted by the Vanqors. There had been a saboteur in their midst. They were afraid they would never make it off-planet.

He understood their testiness, but he wasn't too excited about having to listen to it.

"I think I'll check on Anakin," he said.

The hangar was located in the back, past the utility rooms. There was only one transport and a few speeder bikes that had been dismantled for parts. All Obi-Wan could see were Anakin's legs, sticking out from underneath the transport. Obi-Wan leaned down.

"Any luck?"

Anakin's voice was muffled. "Maybe. But what I wouldn't give for a pit droid."

"Consider me a pit droid," Obi-Wan said. "What can I do?"

Anakin slid out. "You need some servodrivers for hands and a grease pump instead of a nose." He said the words grumpily.

"Well, let me do something," Obi-Wan said. "Have you pinpointed the problem?"

"Sure," Anakin said. "That's the easy part. It's the power generator. The transfer wires from the sublight engine are fused together, which means that the fusion system is completely blown."

"Can you replace the transfer wires?"

"Sure. But then the backup from the power feeds would trigger a response."

"And that response would be . . ."

"The ship would blow up."

"Not optimum," Obi-Wan said.

"I can see where Mezdec tried to improvise. But he keeps running into the same problem." Anakin tapped his finger on the shell of the ship. "Here's what I can't figure," he said. "Why would Samdew disable the ship completely? If he killed all the crew here, how would he get off-planet?"

"Maybe he didn't need the ship," Obi-Wan said. "The Vanqors would pick him up."

"Okay," Anakin said. "But if I were a spy stuck on a remote moon, I'd want a back door, just in case. I wouldn't assume that everything would go as planned."

"Things rarely do." Obi-Wan nodded thoughtfully. "Meaning there must be a way to fix the ship."

"I just don't know what it is yet." Anakin ducked back under the ship. "But I'll find it. Hand me that fuse-cutter, will you?"

Obi-Wan reached for the tool. For the next hour, he silently helped Anakin try one route, then another, to fix the ship. He admired Anakin's focus. It was as though the engine were an ailing organism that he was coaxing back to life.

Mezdec wandered out to help, and he and Anakin conferred. Obi-Wan lost the thread of the conversation, which skimmed over fuse switches, overrides, and surges. He knew something about engines, but not nearly as much as Anakin.

At last Anakin replaced the engine plate, entered the ship, and eased into the pilot seat. He hesitated before firing the engines.

"You might want to back up," he told Obi-Wan, who had also entered the ship.

"How far?"

"To the next star system." Anakin grinned. "Only kidding." He engaged the throttle and the engine roared to life.

Mezdec yelled from the outside, "The kid knows his stuff."

"That he does," Obi-Wan agreed as he exited.

Anakin powered down the engines and leaped out of the ship. "I can get it started, but I can't restore full power. That means no deflector shields. We had to by-pass the weapons delivery system to juice up the gener-ator, so we won't have turbolasers, either. In other words, we'll have a slow ride, and we'll be exposed if the Vanqors track us on radar. And then there's the fuel problem."

"Which is?"

"We don't have much. I ran our options through the computer. The only way to get to Typha-Dor is by the shortest route. That's going to bring us right into Van-qor airspace."

Obi-Wan grimaced. "This just keeps getting better." He looked back at the shelter, where the four crew members waited. "We'll have to risk it. Our only chance is to slip through their surveillance. Space is big."

"Space is big?" A flash of humor made Anakin's eyes sparkle. "That's your strategy? I guess I can stop worrying."

The mischief in Anakin's eyes suddenly lightened Obi-Wan's heart. He saw the flash of a boy he'd once known, a boy who liked to fix things, a boy who had yet to understand the great gifts he had been given. A boy untroubled by those gifts who believed the galaxy would unfold for him, show him the promise of his dreams.

I can't let him lose that spirit. I can't let him lose the boy he was.

He grinned back. "Thanks," he said. "I just thought of it."

As they exchanged smiles, something changed. Something lightened, and the tension between them eased, just a bit.

But then, just as the moment passed, Obi-Wan saw sadness in Anakin's eyes. He caught the same feeling. It was no longer possible to fix things between them with a joke, a light moment. Things ran too deep for that now.

"I'll get the others," Obi-Wan said.

Shalini stood, her hands on her hips, surveying the main room.

"I sure hope you can make that thing take off," she said.

There was nothing left of the shelter. It was now an empty shell. The team's instructions were to destroy anything that could be of use to the Vanqors. Shalini and the rest had used soldering equipment and tools to fuse and destroy the comm and surveillance suites. They had destroyed all their files and everything they could not carry aboard ship.

Anakin sat behind the controls, with Mezdec next to him. "The takeoff could be bumpy," he told the others. "We don't have enough power for a smooth ride. Once we get into the upper atmosphere we should be okay."

Anakin started the engines. The retractable roof of the hangar slid back. Watching the instruments carefully, Anakin gave the engines power and they rose, too slowly for Obi-Wan's comfort. The ship shook with the effort.

Anakin's face was completely calm, but Obi-Wan noted the sheen of perspiration on his skin. The controls shook in his hands. The shuddering ship rose over the icy wasteland. It slid sideways, dangerously close to the side of the mountain. Obi-Wan saw Thik close his eyes. Shalini touched her belt, where the disk lay hidden.

Anakin gave another boost to the power, and the

ship shot up into the upper atmosphere. "That was the hard part," he announced to the others. "Next stop, Typha-Dor."

If we are lucky, Obi-Wan thought. *If we are very, very lucky.*

CHAPTER FOUR

Anakin glanced at the radar. There was no traffic in the vicinity. Most transient ships stayed clear of the Uziel system, due to the troubles there. Now that Vanqor controlled the airspace, no one was eager to tangle with it.

Safe for the moment, Anakin let Rajana take over the piloting. He needed to keep a closer eye on the instruments.

Mezdec looked up from the navigation screen. "Everything all right?"

"I just want to take a look at the stabilizer controls," Anakin said. "Without full power, we'll be in trouble if something malfunctions. I had to reroute the cables from the left stabilizer in order to get lift. I want to make sure we didn't pull too much power on the takeoff. I'm going to run a full status check."

He set the status check in motion and watched as the computer ticked off the different indicators. Anakin decided to do a second check, this time manually. He couldn't be too careful in a ship operating at less than full power. He scanned through the warning sensors.

"That's odd," he said to Mezdec. "I'm getting an indicator green on three power feeds on the escape pod. I'm showing two anti-grav generators."

"The pod does have two anti-grav generators," Mezdec said. "It was upgraded in case it had to be used as a primary transport to get all the way back to Typha-Dor. Samdew sabotaged the pod, too."

"I saw that," Anakin said. "But there was no console indicator for an extra generator and three power feeds."

"The feed indicators are in the pod itself," Mezdec said.

"I see. I'll check them there, then." Anakin went back to the escape pod. He did a status check. Then he stopped by the small area where Obi-Wan had settled himself in the rear of the craft.

Anakin eased into a seat next to him. He leaned over casually and spoke in a low tone. "The escape pod is double-boosted. Highly unusual for this model. The indicators don't run through the sensor array in the main cabin. In other words, I found Samdew's back door. If I'd checked the pod itself, I could have fixed the problem on the transport. All that needed to be done was a rewiring job to suck power from the pod and bring it to the transport. We could have taken off with full power."

"Can you do it now?"

Anakin shook his head. "Not while we're flying. But that's not the issue. I have one question."

"Why didn't Mezdec figure it out?" Obi-Wan interjected in a low tone. "Could it be an oversight?"

Anakin shrugged. "Sure. If he's not very bright. But he seems to know his stuff. And he had a month to try to fix the transport."

Obi-Wan frowned. "Something has been nagging at me. There were scorch marks on the comm console. Mezdec said that he came out of the sleeping quarters and saw Samdew at the comm unit. He saw that Samdew was sending a communication to the Vanqors."

Anakin nodded. "So he blasted the comm console to stop him."

"A blast from that distance shouldn't have left scorch marks on the panel," Obi-Wan said.

"Not unless he shot from very close," Anakin

agreed. "Maybe he was mistaken about where he was standing."

"If he was close enough to blast the panel to leave scorch marks, wouldn't you think he'd be close enough to stop Samdew without shooting? Why did he have a blaster, anyway? He said he'd been sleeping, and it was the middle of the night," Obi-Wan said. "Anyway, the point is that he lied."

"But the others came out and saw what happened," Anakin said. "And Samdew shot Thik."

"Think back, Padawan," Obi-Wan said. "You are telling me the impression you got, not the words that were actually said."

Anakin thought back, annoyed at himself. He had spoken quickly, without reviewing the conversation in his mind. That wasn't consistent with his training.

He focused, as a Jedi should. He remembered the conversation clearly now, in the exact words and sequence the others had used. An exact memory was one of the tools of a Jedi mind.

"Samdew was dying when he tried to shoot Mezdec," Anakin said. "That's what Rajana and Thik saw. Thik just got in the way. So Samdew could have been shooting at Mezdec because *Mezdec* was the spy. But what about Samdew activating the fire system?"

"We only have Mezdec's word for that, too," Obi-Wan

said. "We only have Mezdec's word for everything, including the disabled transport."

"Do you think he's the spy?" Anakin asked.

"I don't know," Obi-Wan said.

Shalini had seen them talking, and she slid into a seat next to Obi-Wan. "Everything all right?"

Anakin glanced at his Master. Mezdec was Shalini's husband. As the head of the group, she had a right to know what they were thinking. But where would her loyalties lie?

"Fine," Obi-Wan said. "Tell us something. Did you have any other evidence that Samdew was the saboteur?"

"What more evidence did we need?" Shalini said. "He killed four of us."

"What do you think his plan was before he was interrupted?" Obi-Wan asked.

"We knew he was beginning his transmission to the Vanqor fleet," Shalini said. "Luckily Mezdec intervened before they got a lock on our position. I imagine that his message would be that we had the invasion plans. Then he would kill us and take off."

"In the disabled transport?"

"The Vanqors would send a transport, I suppose," Shalini said. "What are you suggesting?"

"It seems an inefficient way for a spy to behave,"

Obi-Wan said. "Far better to alert the Vanqors that their plans had been retrieved, then stay in place and hope for more chances to betray Typha-Dor."

"Maybe he was an inefficient spy," Shalini said. "Maybe his mission was over. Maybe he was tired of the cold." She eyed Obi-Wan curiously. "Why don't you say what you mean?"

"There could be another spy," Obi-Wan said. "Or Samdew might have been innocent. He did not get a chance to defend himself."

"He shot Thik!" Shalini said.

"He was aiming at Mezdec," Obi-Wan reminded her. "The only person who had identified him as a spy."

"What are you saying?" Hostility tinged Shalini's words now.

Shalini's voice had risen, and Thik and Olanz looked over. Rajana and Mezdec could not hear.

"We're just going over what happened," Obi-Wan said. "We want to make sure that what you think happened really happened."

"I *know* what happened," Shalini insisted.

"You know what Mezdec told you," Obi-Wan said. "There is a difference. It could be a crucial one. Are you willing to gamble your planet's freedom on your faith in him?"

"Yes," Shalini said with complete certainty.

"I'm not," Olanz said quietly, coming up with Thik. "The Jedi might have a point, Shalini. We are relying on Mezdec for our proof."

Shalini looked at the two of them with disbelief. "Mezdec is not a traitor. He is as loyal to Typha-Dor as I am, as committed to bringing the plans back as I am."

Anakin noticed that she touched her utility belt when she spoke.

"May we see the disk?" he asked.

Shalini looked at him angrily, but she reached into a hidden pocket on her belt and handed Obi-Wan the disk.

Obi-Wan accessed it on his datapad. It was empty of information.

Shalini stared at the disk in shock. "I don't know how . . ."

"Was the disk ever out of your sight?" Obi-Wan asked urgently.

She bit her lip. "No, never. But Mezdec checked my blaster and my emergency supplies on my utility belt before we left. He said he wanted to do it, to make sure I would be safe. . . ." Her voice trailed off. "I have a second disk. I didn't tell Mezdec. The invasion plans are safe."

Rajana's voice rose. "I'm getting radar activity. I think it's a destroyer."

"Where is Mezdec?" Shalini cried. Mezdec had disappeared.

Anakin and Obi-Wan sprang up. "Emergency pod," Obi-Wan said.

They raced to the rear of the ship. Mezdec was accessing the emergency door. He ran inside.

The ship suddenly shook as laser cannonfire erupted. "We're under attack!" Rajana shouted from the cockpit. "I need help here!"

Both Jedi leaped toward the closing door to the escape pod. It locked down before they could reach it.

Obi-Wan swept his lightsaber down the door and the metal peeled back. But he was too late. Mezdec blasted out into space.

CHAPTER FIVE

"We should have been prepared for this," Obi-Wan said.

"He won't get very far very fast," Anakin said. "I disabled half the power. I also cut the comm unit. I'd better get to the pilot seat."

Anakin whirled and charged back toward the cockpit. Obi-Wan followed. Their best chance of escaping the Vanqor bombardment lay with his Padawan at the controls.

Their chances weren't good. At half-power, the ship could not possibly outrun the Vanqor ship, and it would also be hard to maneuver.

Obi-Wan hurried back to the cockpit, where the others stood nervously around Anakin as he took over the controls. The Vanqor ship was behind them, a monster assault ship clad in black and silver. A flash came from the side of the ship.

"Torpedo," Obi-Wan said.

Anakin made a hard right. The ship shuddered as it turned. The torpedo missed them.

Laser cannonfire began to boom. Anakin put the ship into a dive, but Obi-Wan could feel how the ship trembled. He exchanged a look with his apprentice. Anakin's lips thinned. Obi-Wan knew he was determined to get them through. But even Anakin couldn't work miracles. Obi-Wan began to study the map charts, looking for a place to set the ship down.

Unfortunately, the closest planet was Vanqor itself.

"Hang on!" Anakin shouted.

The ship staggered from a direct hit. Blue lightning skittered along the console.

"Ion blast," Anakin said. "We've lost most of our computer systems." He turned the ship again, trying to stay a moving target. He threw a glance at Obi-Wan. "We've got to get the ship down."

Obi-Wan looked at the others. "Our only choice is Vanqor."

The group exchanged glances. They had been through so much and accomplished so much. Landing on Vanqor and being captured could mean the end for all of them. But when they turned to Obi-Wan, not one of them looked afraid.

"If it is our only choice, let us take it," Thik said.

Anakin dipped the ship into the planet's atmosphere. "Can you give me a coordinate?" he asked Obi-Wan. "I don't have much time to maneuver, but I'll do what I can."

Obi-Wan didn't have time to consult the onboard references. He thought back on the holomaps he had studied. "Our best chance of evading capture is to land on the outskirts of the Tomo Craters," he said. "It's rugged terrain. We might be able to lose them there, if you can guide us to a safe landing." Obi-Wan quickly sat down at the computer and brought up the coordinates.

Anakin nodded briefly, too intent on keeping the ship on course to waste any movement. The ship rocked and shuddered under his hands. Suddenly it began to list to one side.

"The left stabilizer is failing," he muttered. "Everyone strap in. We're going to have to crash-land."

Vanqor loomed below, a large, multicolored planet. Obi-Wan knew from his research that it was primarily made up of deserts and dry, high plateaus. Cities were midsize and strung out along the few fertile valleys. The Tomo Craters area was a remote section that thousands of years ago had been hit by a meteor shower. Deep craters and fissures marked the dry land.

Suddenly an alarm began to sound. Red lights flashed in the cockpit. Another bank of lights lit up. Anakin didn't say a word. He didn't have to. Everyone knew what it meant: The ship was failing.

Instead of slowing, Anakin pushed his speed. Obi-Wan admired his cool. He knew what Anakin was counting on. The faster they got down, the better. He just wasn't sure what would happen when they got closer. Anakin would try to hug the surface, hiding from the ship above until he could land. Normally, Anakin would relish this challenge and perform it flawlessly. But with a wounded ship, he was taking big chances.

Obi-Wan prepared himself. They passed over a green valley, and Anakin brought the ship closer to the surface. The entire frame was shaking. Sirens blared and red lights flashed. The surface loomed closer. Red dirt was kicked up by their turbulence. It looked as though they were about to crash into boulders as big as buildings. The ship rolled to one side, nearly sending them into a massive rock formation. Anakin corrected it. Sweat beaded his upper lip.

Obi-Wan saw a smooth plateau ahead. Anakin would try to land there. He slowed his speed, and the ship wobbled, rolling from side to side. If they hadn't strapped in, they would have been flung against the walls.

"I've lost the left stabilizer completely!" Anakin shouted. "Hang on!"

The ship slammed into the unforgiving ground. Obi-Wan felt his body rise up as though it weighed nothing. He came down, jarring teeth and bones. He tasted blood in his mouth. The ship careened down the plateau, tearing chunks of vegetation and knocking into small boulders. The noise was tremendous. The ship suddenly seemed a fragile thing, shaking so hard Obi-Wan wondered if it would simply fall to pieces.

The end of the plateau was less than fifty meters away. If the ship didn't stop moving, they would careen right off it, straight into the canyon bottom hundreds of meters below. Anakin frantically worked the controls. Obi-Wan saw the lip of the plateau approach. Slowly, slowly, the ship began to slide. A terrible groaning noise, worse than the harsh grating of the crash, rose in the air around them, battering their ears like a physical force. The ship suddenly tipped almost all the way to one side, slamming Obi-Wan against the console.

Then the ship crashed against a boulder and stopped.

Obi-Wan looked around. Thik looked pale. No doubt the bumpy landing had been hard on his injury. Shalini's forehead was bleeding. Olanz and Rajana looked shaken but all right.

"We've got to get out of here fast," Obi-Wan said.

He unbuckled himself and Anakin did the same. They helped the others to quickly extricate themselves from their seats. The landing ramp wouldn't engage, and the door had been mangled from the landing. Obi-Wan and Anakin set to work with their lightsabers to cut a hole through the hull.

Anakin suddenly stopped. He bent over to look through the viewport. "They must have contacted Vanqor planetary security. Guard ships are approaching," he said. "They've located us."

"Do you have any smoke grenades and air masks aboard?" Obi-Wan asked Shalini.

"I'll get them," Rajana said. She hurried down the aisle of the ship, holding on to seat backs to stay upright.

Obi-Wan spoke even as they continued to peel back the hull with their lightsabers. "Our best chance is to launch down that canyon on cables. Anakin, you take Shalini and Olanz. I'll take Thik and Rajana. We'll use the smoke grenades for cover. Turn on your tracking device in case we lose each other."

The hole was big enough now. Obi-Wan tossed out two smoke grenades. The acrid smoke billowed out.

Without much wind, the smoke hung in the air, a perfect cover. One by one, wearing air masks to protect their lungs, they slid through the hole.

They were still out of range of the starship's weapons. They had only minutes now. They began to run toward the edge of the plateau.

Shaken from the landing, some of the group could not move fast. Thik, with his bad knee, was especially slow. Obi-Wan and Anakin helped them along, but within seconds, Obi-Wan did a quick calculation and realized they couldn't make it. The starships could begin shooting through the smoke at any moment. The Vanqors might not be able to pinpoint their location, but they certainly could figure out where they were headed. It was the only avenue of escape.

Obi-Wan felt desperate. The question was, would the ships try to kill them or take them prisoner?

They couldn't see the starships, but the first fire tore up the ground in front of them. They jumped back. The fire was constant, preventing them from reaching the edge of the plateau.

"Back to the ship!" Obi-Wan called. It would at least offer some cover.

They ran, the fire behind them now. Shalini tripped, but Anakin picked her up and dove underneath the belly of the ship. Thik was still moving too slowly. He was not keeping up with the others and would be a prime target when the smoke cleared. Obi-Wan grabbed him. He ran forward to push Thik into an empty space where crushed metal had created a cubbyhole.

He saw too late that there was only room for one. Obi-Wan pushed Thik into the space and kept on going. The smoke was starting to clear. Obi-Wan dived for a boulder and took shelter behind it. He was wedged in between the boulder and a larger one behind him. There was barely room, but he doubted he could be seen from above.

The starships landed. The group huddled under their own ship. Obi-Wan saw Shalini move toward Anakin. She handed him something and spoke rapidly in his ear.

The disk. She had handed him the disk.

Obi-Wan realized that the Vanqors had decided on capture. They could have easily blown up the ship by now if they'd wanted.

Dozens of troops exited their ship. A squad headed for the downed ship while another peeled off to search the area.

Obi-Wan searched his hiding place. He realized that if he could squeeze a bit further behind the boulder, it opened up into a small cavelike opening impossible to see unless you were right on top of it. It offered a perfect place to hide.

He could not do them any good by being captured too. It tore at him to leave his Padawan, but it was his only hope.

He squeezed back into the hole, then doubled over to fit himself into the space. From here he could see through a crevice in the rock out to the ship.

Soldiers rounded up the group and herded them onto their starships. Obi-Wan's heart ached. There was no way he and Anakin alone could fend off dozens of soldiers and well-armed enemy ships.

The starships took off and shot away into the distance. Slowly, Obi-Wan hauled himself up. He panted out his exhaustion and his frustration.

Then he made himself stand and turned his thoughts toward rescue.

The soldiers had bound their hands behind them and pushed them aboard the starships. Anakin felt the disk burn against his skin. So far he had not been searched, but he would use the Force to divert attention. Shalini had entrusted the disk to him, and he wouldn't fail her.

She had spoken rapidly in his ear. "Take this. It will be safest in the hands of the Jedi. For the safety of my people, please get it back to Typha-Dor."

"I pledge my life on it," Anakin had said.

The starships flew over the deep fissures of the Tomo Craters. On the lip of a crater, a small compound huddled. Out of the viewport, Anakin glimpsed gray buildings, energy fences, security towers, and a small landing pad.

"Welcome to paradise," one of the soldiers snickered. "The Tomo Camp."

Dressed in his survival suit like the others, with his lightsaber safely hidden, Anakin was not identified as a Jedi. Shalini refused to give her name, along with the others. The admitting guard didn't seem to care. They were searched, but Anakin was able to use the Force to confuse his guard, and his cable launcher, his lightsaber, and the disk were not taken. They were stripped of their survival gear and given rough brown tunics to wear. Then they were herded out into a small yard surrounded by energy fencing. The wind was cold and tore at their clothes. Around them swirled other prisoners from other worlds in the Uziel system, planets already conquered by Vanqor.

Anakin looked around. The walls of the crater were sheer and hundreds of meters tall. It was clear that the only way into the camp was by air.

How would Obi-Wan rescue him? The ship had been destroyed in the crash.

The answer was that Obi-Wan most likely would not be able to get to him. It was all up to Anakin. Anakin did not mind this knowledge. He didn't mind depending on his own skill.

He had a time limit. Shalini had told them that the invasion was due in only three days. He would have to find a way to escape soon. The key to the survival of the entire planet of Typha-Dor lay hidden in his tunic pocket. He had managed to conceal the disk from the guards, but he didn't kid himself that he would be able to evade the heavy security measures by the Force alone.

He had made the mistake once of thinking he was more powerful than he was. He would never do it again. He would not make a move until he was sure.

An Uziel prisoner in a faded uniform drifted near them. "What's the news? Have the Vanqors invaded Typha-Dor?"

Shalini's eyes glinted. "No. And if they do, we will drive them back."

The prisoner looked weary. "That's what we said on Zilior."

"Have there been any escape attempts here?" Shalini asked.

"One. He's dead. My advice is to accept your fate." The prisoner drifted away.

"I make my own fate," Shalini said to her cohorts. She looked at Anakin. "Do you have any ideas?"

"Not yet," Anakin said easily, sitting down on the cold ground.

"What are you doing?" Shalini asked. "Aren't you going to do something?"

"I am," Anakin said. Tuning out the others, he began to watch.

There was only one solution. Anakin had to get to the transport pool. The question was when. There were four groups of guards on eight-hour shifts, so that over-lap guaranteed that one group was always relatively fresh. In addition, sentry droids constantly buzzed the compound. It wasn't impossible. But it would take the right timing.

Anakin still had his lightsaber and his cable launcher. He could launch over the energy fence, but then he would have to cross thirty meters of open space to get to the transport pool. The transports were heavily guarded, but not the ones needing repair. If he made it to the repair shed, he could slip inside. He would just have to hope that he could fix a transport and take off before his absence was noted.

He couldn't take the others. He would have to escape alone, and hope to return for them.

There was no sense waiting. He would escape that night.

The gate door slid back. An officer entered, surrounded by guards and droids. He began to walk through the crowd as the prisoners shrank back.

"What's going on?" Shalini whispered.

"A sweep," a prisoner muttered next to her. "They come every few weeks and take several of us."

"No one ever comes back," someone else murmured. "They take them to an unmarked building. There are rumors of medical experiments."

The officer pointed a finger at one prisoner, then another. The guards surrounded them and herded them together.

Then the officer wheeled about and pointed directly at Anakin. "Him."

"No," Shalini whispered.

Anakin considered resisting. With a glance at the others the guards had herded together, he decided he could not. He knew that if a battle ensued, others would die.

And there were reasons to submit. Security could be a bit more lax at the facility where they were taking him. Anakin fell into step behind the others.

They were led to a gray building with no sign outside. When they were ushered inside, Anakin's nose twitched. It smelled like chemicals. So the rumors could be true. The prisoners exchanged uneasy glances.

They were prodded along the hallway and pushed into a bare white room. There a holoscreen took up an entire wall. An image of a human male dressed in a med coat appeared on the screen. He smiled gently.

"Do not fear. You will not be harmed. On the contrary, you are about to enjoy the experience for which we have chosen you. Welcome to the Zone of Self-Containment. A doctor will be with you shortly to explain. In the meantime, relax."

"Relax," one of the prisoners snorted. "Good advice, med-head."

The holo image blinked off.

"What did he say?" another one of the imprisoned soldiers asked. "The Zone of Self-Containment? What are they going to do to us?" He pressed his fingers to his forehead. "I feel strange."

Anakin, too, felt light-headed. He suddenly realized why the information had been given to them by a holo image instead of a real person.

"The room is filled with some kind of gas. They've drugged us," he said as his vision blurred. He felt his knees turn to water. One of the prisoners slumped to the floor.

Anakin felt himself slipping downward. He fought the sensation of the gas. The others slipped into unconsciousness. He held himself in readiness. He tried to move his legs and found that they were too heavy.

He was the only one conscious when the technicians entered the room in masks. He saw, but he could not move a finger. The technicians began to load the other prisoners onto repulsorlift stretchers.

"Look at this one, he's still awake," one of the technicians said, drawing closer to Anakin. "Never seen that before."

"He's not too happy about being here, either," another said.

One of them leaned closer to Anakin. "Don't fight it, friend. We just want some cooperation in the beginning. I guarantee you'll like your stay here."

Using every ounce of his will and strength, Anakin grabbed the technician by the collar and brought his face even closer. "Don't . . . bet . . . on it."

The technician yelped and struggled to free himself. "Help! For galaxy's sake!"

The other two rushed over. Anakin could not fight the three of them. He was thrown onto the stretcher and strapped down. He dipped in and out of consciousness as the stretcher was powered down the hall. A door opened. The light hurt his eyes.

They began to undress him. *My lightsaber,* Anakin thought. *The disk.* He had retained his utility belt and concealed the disk inside a hidden slit. He had concealed his lightsaber by lodging it against his body underneath the tunic, strapping the belt tight against the hilt.

He could not summon the Force enough to distract the technicians from finding it. He was helpless. Only luck could save him from discovery. The belt was unstrapped and hit the tiled floor with a soft thud. His tunic followed. The technician scooped up the bundle and tossed it in a storage box with clothes from the other prisoners.

Anakin shut his eyes against the harsh light. He felt himself being lifted and slipped into water. He tried to fight, afraid he would drown.

"Relax, friend," the technician said. "It's just a bath."

The water was warm. He slid against the side. He was strapped in so that his head wouldn't slip beneath the surface. Anakin's mind drifted as though he were floating off on a deep, dark lake.

He must have slept. When he woke, he was dry and was wearing a fresh tunic, this one a soft material, in dark blue. He was lying on a sleep couch. The sleep had refreshed him. He felt relaxed and energized. He stretched, marveling at how fluid his limbs felt. The paralyzing drug effects had worn off, but strangely, had left him feeling limber.

He recognized the technician who handed him a pillow. "Feel better? Told you so. Almost time for the evening meal."

Anakin shook his head.

"They all refuse at first," the med technician said. "Don't worry, the food isn't drugged. We all eat together, workers and patients."

Anakin shrugged. Maybe the man was telling the truth. Maybe not. Oddly, Anakin didn't care. It was as though cool water had run through his veins, calming every impulse, every desire.

He walked to the dining hall. Tables were set up, and other patients and med workers were eating. There was a long table with platters heaped with fruits and vegetables, pastries and meats. Anakin saw that everyone ate from the same plates, so he took some food and ate it.

He chewed, wondering what would come next. He supposed something would happen soon. When it did, he would react.

The need to help Typha-Dor seemed so distant now. Someone else would help the planet. There was always someone else to do something, if you waited. He would just pass the time here and see what the Vanqors were up to. That could be valuable to the Typha-Dor, too. He needn't worry about the invasion right now.

He ate and followed some other prisoners out into the courtyard. Warming lights had been set up, and the air was comfortable. Flowers grew, and large, leafy trees. Anakin found a bench and sat. He felt something he had not felt in a long, long time, not since he was a little boy nestled in his mother's embrace: peace.

I'll fight it soon. When I need to escape, I will. But right now . . . right now, would it be so wrong to enjoy it?

CHAPTER SEVEN

Obi-Wan waited until the starships were out of sight. He couldn't risk a long transmission to the Temple. But he would have to risk a distress call. The calls would be coded and scrambled, and he would have to hope it could reach the Temple.

They could lock on his position and send help. It would take almost two days to arrive, but he had to risk it.

The tracking device tucked in Anakin's tunic beeped a steady signal. Obi-Wan trudged back to the ship. He climbed through the hole and went to the rear cargo hold. He had to cut through the crunched door with his lightsaber. He remembered that they had loaded one swoop aboard. They had to leave the rest behind because Anakin needed to lighten the ship's load as much as possible.

The swoop was dented from slamming back and forth between the cargo hold's walls, but it still worked. Anakin had made sure of that before they left the outpost. Now he had transportation. Obi-Wan only hoped that Anakin was close enough to get to on a swoop. It was small, built for short distances, and it didn't hold much fuel.

He climbed aboard and took off. The tracking device led him over the high plateaus and desert lands surrounding the Tomo Craters. He looked down as he sped over the terrain, glad he wasn't on foot. The plateaus were high and steep, and trails led to dead ends and switchbacks. It would have taken days to traverse the distance. Obi-Wan stayed as close to the ground as he dared, trying to evade scanners and surveillance from above. The tracking device led him on as the sun slid lower in the sky.

The fuel read EMPTY and the engine began to sputter. By Obi-Wan's reckoning he was still at least twenty kilometers from Anakin. He had no choice. He had to land.

He pulled the swoop into a cave, entering the coordinates on his datapad. He might need it later, if he could find some fuel. He started to walk.

It was hard going. Obi-Wan hiked up and down steep slopes of thin rock shale that occasionally broke into dangerous rockslides. At last he stopped to rest when the source of the tracking device's transmission was in sight.

Obi-Wan studied the camp through his electrobinoculars. The good news was that the perimeter security wasn't heavy, most likely because the camp relied on its inaccessibility.

He had reached the heart of the Tomo Craters. A careful survey of the ground made Obi-Wan conclude that camp security was correct not to worry about escaping prisoners. If Obi-Wan could manage to scramble up and down cliffs and hike through canyons without disturbing a nest of gundarks or getting attacked by various other horrifying creatures, he *might* make it to the outskirts of the camp. Then he would have to scale a sheer rock wall two hundred meters high. He would be vulnerable with every centimeter he traveled. It would be better to go in by air.

Of course, he didn't have a transport. That could be a problem.

He sat on a high peak, underneath an outcropping of rocks. He watched the camp operations for the rest of the waning evening. Transports flew in and out in a regular pattern, ferrying supplies and possibly carrying troops back and forth. Obi-Wan guessed that the camp must also be a base of some sort.

He could wait for a few days to see if his message had reached the Temple. But what if it hadn't?

Rescue was his first priority. He had to get that disk to Typha-Dor.

And if Anakin didn't have the disk, what would you do? If Shalini had given it to you, would you take it to Typha-Dor and abandon him?

The answer should have been easy. As a Jedi, his commitment was to the galaxy. He would have had to go to Typha-Dor without Anakin. Would he have attempted a rescue anyway, knowing that Anakin would be waiting for him? He was glad he didn't have to make that choice.

The flight pattern of the ships was always the same. They dipped low as they came in, then landed close to the edge of the plateau, where a short landing pad was surrounded by energy fencing.

Obi-Wan surveyed the area carefully. He thought back on the beginning of the mission, when he'd been brooding about how careful he had become, how much he now weighed risks and thought things through.

Well, he had thought things through, and he had decided that this plan was crazy. He could get pummeled by rocks. He could crash into a crater hundreds of meters below. He could be spotted and blasted into thin air.

All of these scenarios were likely. It was a risky plan. It bordered on stupid.

Which meant that perhaps he wasn't so careful after all.

CHAPTER EIGHT

Once, Anakin and Obi-Wan had taken a few weeks to travel through the grasslands of the planet Belazura, strictly for pleasure. Obi-Wan considered the planet to be among the most beautiful in the galaxy, and he wanted to show it to Anakin. Anakin remembered Obi-Wan telling him that even the life of the Jedi must include time to reflect among beautiful surroundings. Anakin's only instructions during the trip were to enjoy himself. He had.

He had seen fields of grasses that ranged from light sunny yellows to deep greens. He had seen golden fields dotted with deep red flowers. Blue skies had surrounded them like a halo of light. He remembered that he was never hot, and never cold. That the breeze against his skin had felt as soft as his mother's touch.

It had been a peaceful time he had returned to

again and again in his daydreams. And now he was experiencing it once more.

To Anakin's surprise, he underwent no treatments. He was not drugged again. He was not treated like a prisoner. His room was spare, with just a sleep couch and table, but he had access to a sunny area inside and the courtyard outside. Anakin found that he wanted nothing more than to sit there, his face tilted to the warming lights, watching the shadow patterns of the leaves on the wall. He found that it was easy to contemplate the different greens of the leaves for hours. Yet it was not the mindlessness of the meditation he had been taught. He did not leave his body. He did not leave his cares. He could see them as though they were off at a distance. They had nothing to do with him. He knew that everything would work out as it should.

He was not sure how much time had passed. Maybe no more than a day or two. Anakin occasionally thought about escaping. The thought would drift across his mind like a warm breeze, and then disappear.

One afternoon two med technicians came into the garden and stood before him. "Someone would like to see you, Prisoner 42601."

Anakin rose and followed them. He felt a slight curiosity. They walked on either side of him, not touching him or restraining him in any way. There was no need to.

Anakin was led into an office. The technicians left, shutting the door quietly behind them. Unlike the rest of the complex, which was comfortable but spare, this office was full of color and luxury. A thick, patterned carpet was on the floor and septsilk curtains in deep blue hung at the windows. He thought he could smell a pleasant perfume. He sat down in a soft chair and leaned back against a rose-colored pillow.

A human woman walked into the room. Her blond hair was threaded with silver and coiled at the nape of her neck. She was older, he sensed, but he could not tell by her face, which was unlined and smooth. Her eyes were penetrating but warm.

Instead of sitting behind the desk, she perched on the edge of it. "Thank you for coming."

Anakin nodded. He could hear a ghost in his head, a murmur of the person he had been. That person would have said, *Did I have a choice?* But now he did not feel like challenging this person, this woman with the pretty hair and the warm smile.

"I asked to see you," she said. "I am the doctor who invented the Zone of Self-Containment. You have seen that we haven't lied to you. Your experience is about pleasure, not pain. I have a theory that if you are surrounded by pleasant things and no worries, your mind will elevate to that level. Are you happy here?"

Anakin considered the question. Happy? Suddenly he felt confused. What did the word mean? Had he ever been happy? He remembered a flash of a young boy, running home through narrow streets. He remembered laughing with his friend Tru Veld, a fellow Padawan who he had not seen in a year. He could locate the memory, but not the feeling.

For some reason, his confusion made her smile. "Wrong question. Let me rephrase. Are you content?"

That he could answer. "Yes."

"Good. That is our goal. Now. The reason I asked for you is that the technicians tell me that you were able to fight the paralyzing agent we used when you first arrived. I should explain that the agent is used only to allay any anxiety you might feel. Naturally as prisoners of war you would suspect that something terrible might happen to you. The agent was only used to make the experience more comfortable for you. You needed to be bathed and dressed, and the paralyzer allowed us to do that without you or the technicians getting hurt. It was for everyone's benefit, you see."

That seemed reasonable, but Anakin said nothing. Although he was perfectly content to talk to this doctor, and was enjoying this wonderful peace he felt, being here had not completely erased the memory of being a Jedi. He did not necessarily trust what this doctor had to say.

"It is impossible to resist that paralyzing gas, yet you assaulted a technician."

"I grabbed his collar," Anakin corrected pleasantly.

"And you spoke to him."

"It seemed appropriate under the circumstances."

She nodded in appreciation. "I see that though you are in the zone, you still have your wits about you."

"I don't like to abandon them completely, no," Anakin offered.

She studied him now. Anakin could feel sunlight touch his face. His skin warmed, and he wanted to close his eyes to enjoy the sensation, but he didn't.

"I feel something in you," she said. "There is a mastery of your body, of your mind. I've seen it before. Have you ever heard of the Force?"

Anakin did not show by a flick of muscle that the question had startled him. His Jedi training ran deeper than anything else. He felt it stir, and he leaned into it for support. "No."

She nodded again, slightly. "That may be true, and it may not. If you don't know it already, you might be Force-sensitive. That means you could have special abilities."

Wary now, Anakin shrugged. He didn't want to discuss the Force with this woman. He wanted to go back to the garden. The quickest way to do this, he knew, was to seem bored by her questions.

"Did you ever see something happen before it actually happened?" she asked.

He made himself look blank. "I don't think so."

"Are your reaction times unusually fast? Do you have an unusually strong focus?"

He took a long pause that stretched for a moment. She leaned forward in anticipation.

"Uh, what was the question?"

She made an impatient gesture. "*Were* your reaction times unusually fast? Before you came here."

"I was always the first to reach the table for a meal."

She leaned back, disappointed. Her eyes went blank. It was as though now that she was bored with him, he didn't exist.

"You can go back to the garden now."

Anakin stood and left the room. He walked back to the courtyard. The doctor was working for the Vanqors. She wasn't a native Vanqor. Vanqors were humans, but they all dressed in gray tunics and didn't adorn their clothing. She was an outlander, no question.

There was a time he would have been on fire to discover who she was and why she was here. But today the sun shone, and it was warm in the courtyard. And it was almost time for the midday meal.

CHAPTER NINE

Even with the help of the cable launcher, it took Obi-Wan hours to scale the peak. The sun was setting as he reached the top and sat down to rest under a rock outcropping that had created a small cave. He would need all his strength for his task.

Over the wide chasm below, he saw the camp. He was close enough to see without electrobinoculars beings moving about. He watched as a small transport came toward him. He knew he could not be seen, so he was able to study the flight line of the ship. It buzzed overhead, seeming close enough to touch, then zoomed down to land at the camp landing platform.

Obi-Wan fingered his cable launcher. If he timed it exactly right, he should be able to hook onto the underside of a low-flying transport. They wouldn't be able to feel the drag for that short a distance. He would let himself be towed by the transport and then drop to the ground during the landing. If everything went right.

If something went wrong, he'd be squashed like a bug against the side of a crater.

He rolled himself up into his thermal cape and told himself to go to sleep. Worrying about Anakin would only interfere with the rest he needed. Yet the sky turned black and many stars had appeared before he felt sleep overtake him.

He smelled the dawn in his sleep before he woke. The freshness of the air infiltrated his dreams, and when he opened his eyes he felt hopeful.

He stretched in the chill, trying to warm his muscles. He munched on a protein cube as he made his preparations. He tested the cable several times. His life depended on its strength.

Trust your materials, but test them twice.

Yes, Qui-Gon.

The first transport came in too high. The second, too fast. Obi-Wan crouched in the shadow of the rocks. Patience was necessary. He couldn't make a mistake.

The next transport came in low and kept reducing speed. It was a midsize cruiser, big enough that it would not feel the jolt of the launcher or the drag of his body — he hoped. He didn't think he'd get a better opportunity.

As the shadow of the cruiser touched the peak, Obi-Wan aimed and sent the cable flying. It latched onto the underbelly of the ship. He was yanked upward with such force he nearly lost consciousness. He had expected a bad jolt, but not this bad. With the wind whistling past his ears and his body whirling and flopping, he tried to get his hands around the cable. He had to steady himself if this was going to work.

His arms were nearly wrenched from their sockets as he held onto the cable. He tucked his knees up and his chin down. He kept his finger on the cable control. He brought himself up closer to the body of the ship, knowing he couldn't get too close or he'd be burned by the exhausts as the ship began to land.

A boulder loomed ahead. He activated the launcher to get closer to the ship. He zoomed up as the rock approached, passing under him by a few meters. He activated the launcher to drop him again, out of reach of the rocket exhaust. He couldn't be this close when the ship began to land or he'd be burned to a cinder.

A large rock formation appeared out of nowhere. Obi-Wan quickly tucked his legs up, but the ship bumped on an air current and his shoulder slammed against the rock. Pain shot through him. He held on. The ship banked, nearly slamming him into a cliff wall.

Maybe this wasn't such a smart idea.

The muscles in his arms and legs began to shake, and his fingers clenched in the effort to hold on to the cable.

Obi-Wan called on the Force to help him. He was part of the ship, part of the air, part of the cable itself. He would move when he needed to move, he would allow the grace of the ship to pull him to a safe landing. . . .

The pilot of the transport apparently liked to show off. He dipped the transport sideways and wagged its wings. Obi-Wan was whipped from side to side.

Safe landing? I'll be lucky if I make it without being squashed.

The landing platform was ahead. He would have to drop off quickly, very close to the perimeter wall. If not, he could be spotted.

The ship slowed and dipped. Obi-Wan counted out the seconds. At the last possible moment, he disengaged the cable. Bracing himself, he fell through the air, landing hard. He felt the jolt up to his eyebrows. He rolled and ducked behind a parked ship.

He caught his breath as the ship he had hitched a

ride on came to a stop. Droids began to unload cargo. He saw a small utility shed nearby and quickly headed for it.

The shed held tools and equipment. Obi-Wan searched and was glad to find what he was looking for, a bin full of greasy coveralls. He pulled a pair on. Then he quickly darted out of the shed. His surveillance through his electrobinoculars had given him a rough outline of the camp. He knew the prisoners filed out into the yard at this time. There was always some confusion as they poured out of the buildings. He couldn't have arrived at a better time.

He walked briskly across the landing pad as if he belonged there. Then he struck out toward the fenced yard. He had tucked a servodriver in his pocket, and he pretended to be checking the energy fence as he moved down, searching the crowd for Anakin.

He saw Shalini. She sat, removed from the others, close to the fence. Her head was bowed and her hands were clasped in front of her. He made his way down the length of the fence toward her.

She lifted her head as he came near. At first she didn't see him. Her gaze passed over him, just another one of her captors, as she sought the sky. Then she jerked her gaze back to him. Obi-Wan admired her discipline. She gave no sign that she had recognized him.

Instead she casually scooted back until she was closer to the fence. She absently drew in the dirt with a finger, looking casual.

"Is everyone all right?" Obi-Wan asked, bending over with the servodriver.

"Yes. But Anakin has been taken away. No one knows why."

"Where?"

"There is a gray building across the compound. Unmarked. He was taken there. Listen, they don't know who we are yet. They don't know he's a Jedi. Which makes me think."

He was anxious to find Anakin, but Obi-Wan bent closer to hear what Shalini would say. "If Mezdec had gone straight to Vanqor, he would be there by now. He would have told them we were traveling in Vanqor airspace and they would have figured out who we are. Which tells me that Mezdec didn't go to Vanqor."

"Where do you think he went?"

"I think he went to Typha-Dor. He would assume that either we had been captured or we were still making our way there."

"But why would he go to Typha-Dor?"

"To deliver the invasion plans. But not the real ones."

Obi-Wan let out a breath. "Of course. They would accept whatever he would bring as real."

"He will destroy us single-handedly," Shalini said, her voice raw. "All is lost."

"No," Obi-Wan said. "If we can make it in time —"

"Anakin has the disk. You must get it —"

"You there!" An angry voice cut through Shalini's words. "Attendance check!"

"Find him and go. Don't worry about us. Save Typha-Dor."

Shalini rose and walked off, unwilling to risk exposing Obi-Wan.

Obi-Wan tucked the servodriver in his pocket and went off in search of the building Shalini had indicated. He knew from experience that wearing dirty coveralls and affecting a purposeful stride would render him close to invisible.

He found the building and decided his best course was to walk right in. He was making up his plans now as he went along, counting on his connection to the Force to guide him. He found himself in a small vestibule. A security checkpoint was just inside the plain durasteel door.

"Checking on those valves in the air handlers," Obi-Wan said.

The officer looked down at his datascreen. "I didn't get an alert."

Obi-Wan shrugged. "I'll come back. They probably won't blow."

The officer nodded, then did a double take. "Hold on. Probably?"

Obi-Wan shrugged again.

The officer sighed. "I'm not going to get blamed for this one. Come on in." He pressed a button, deactivating the security shield. Obi-Wan strolled in, as though he had all the time in the world.

As soon as he was out of sight, he walked rapidly down the corridors, looking in open doors and observation windows. Many of the rooms were empty. He rounded a corner and saw a pair of double doors. Through a window he saw a courtyard dappled with sunlight.

He drew closer to the window. Anakin sat on a bench, his hands in his lap. He didn't appear to have been abused. He wasn't in pain. Nothing about him had altered, and yet . . . he looked different somehow.

Something was wrong. Something was off. And Obi-Wan didn't have time to analyze it. He had to get Anakin out of here.

CHAPTER TEN

Anakin was thinking about detachment. It was the goal of Jedi training. It was a discipline that took years to learn. It was not about controlling emotion, but allowing it to flow through you.

Well, he certainly felt detached. He knew somehow he had been drugged, his brain chemistry altered, even though he wasn't sure how it had been done. Was this how it felt, he wondered, to be truly one with the Force? It was a peaceful place to be, so unlike the battles he usually fought in his mind and heart. Was it so terrible to reach this place through a simple procedure, rather than through years of study and trial? He had admired Obi-Wan's serenity, had envied it. Now he had it. Why did he feel that Obi-Wan would not value it?

The flash of irritation he felt at his Master was gone

in a moment, almost before he had felt it. Anakin smiled. That was certainly something he was unable to do on his own. Being able to think about his Master without emotion was an interesting experience.

Sunlight flashed on the double doors. Someone was entering the garden. At first the sun was in his eyes. Then he saw that it was his Master, dressed in coveralls. No doubt he had come to rescue him. Anakin noted that he should feel glad. Yet he did not. Did he feel disappointed? He couldn't locate an actual feeling.

"Anakin? Are you all right?" Obi-Wan's voice was low.

"I'm fine," he said.

"We have to get out of here. I have a way out."

"That's good." It was good that Obi-Wan had a way out. Anakin stood. He moved with the same alertness he always had, but something was different. It was as though he was watching himself from above.

Yet how good it was to fall into step beside Obi-Wan. Good because he felt so peaceful. How pleasant it was to be Obi-Wan's companion and yet not worry about the emotion connected with that.

Obi-Wan peered into his face. "What did they do to you?"

Anakin decided at that moment that he must not tell his Master what had been done to him. There was no reason to. No doubt the effect would wear off soon, and until then he wanted to spin out the peace he'd found without Obi-Wan judging how he'd found it.

"Nothing." Technically, this was true. He'd received no drugs that he knew about. "I suppose they had plans for us."

Obi-Wan gave him a quick look, as though he didn't believe him. But they didn't have time to stop.

Obi-Wan led him to a utility closet. There, he gave Anakin a medic's pale blue coat. "Do you still have the disk?"

The disk. How odd that he hadn't thought of it. But Obi-Wan had, of course. Was that why his Master had come? For the disk. Not for him. There had been a time when he would have pondered on this, and the thought would have given him pain.

Anakin wrenched his mind back to Obi-Wan's question. It seemed to take more effort than it should to remember what had happened to the disk.

"I know where it is. It's with my lightsaber."

Obi-Wan gave him an odd look. "And where is that?"

"Where we bathe. There are storage bins."

"Show me."

Obi-Wan followed behind Anakin so that it would not seem that they were together. Anakin led him into the room with the large tubs. It was empty. He walked to the storage bin, which was jumbled with the same tunics and belts.

"In here."

With a sound of exasperation, Obi-Wan plunged his hands into the bin. He sorted through the tunics and belts. Anakin bent over to help. He found his belt and removed the disk. Obi-Wan handed Anakin his lightsaber. Then he took the disk from Anakin and slipped it inside his tunic.

"Once we get out of here, we'll head straight for the landing pad," Obi-Wan said crisply. "We're going to have to steal a transport. Can you do that?"

Why was Obi-Wan talking to him as though he were a fourth-year student? "Of course."

"Follow me then."

Obi-Wan led the way. As they approached the security desk, Obi-Wan began talking loudly.

"If I say that the valve shutoff is broken, then it's broken. There's no need to talk to my superior." Obi-Wan rolled his eyes at the security officer. "He's going to tell you the same thing I said. I said, it's broken, you have to shut down the system. If you want to know about a bacta bath, go to a medic. If you want to know about valves, come to me. Understand?" Obi-Wan kept talking as the security guard released the security shield. Obi-Wan activated the door and waited for Anakin to walk through. "He's going to say the same thing. You have to shut down the system. . . ."

The door hissed closed behind them. Obi-Wan headed down the path. Anakin strode next to him. He was content to follow his Master's plan.

No one stopped them as they walked across the compound and moved onto the landing pad.

"This looks fast." Obi-Wan climbed up on a small starship. "We need something that can get us to Typha-Dor." He accessed the cockpit and jumped in. "Let's go, Anakin."

Anakin leaped up on the starship and slid into the cockpit next to his Master. He looked at the controls. "I'm going to have to hot-wire it," he said.

"That's the idea," Obi-Wan answered.

Anakin opened the sensor panel. Even though he still existed in the bubble of his calm, he remembered exactly what to do. He switched wires and juiced the ignition. Then he closed the panel and slid back into the pilot's seat. The engine started on the first try.

"Great," Obi-Wan said with relief. "Let's get out of here. Now," he added urgently, as a security officer began to wave frantically at them. No doubt he assumed they'd forgotten the departure check proceedings.

Anakin eased the throttle. The graceful ship rose, and he shot away from the camp.

Obi-Wan let out an audible sigh. "Things aren't usually that easy."

Anakin glanced at the cockpit indicators. "They aren't this time, either. Apparently by hot-wiring the ship, we skipped an essential step in the procedure."

A red light was blinking on the console. Obi-Wan leaned forward. "What's that?"

"We should have entered a code on the ground. It's a system to prevent escapes, I guess."

"And what is it?" Obi-Wan asked impatiently.

"The ship is programmed to self-destruct," Anakin answered.

CHAPTER ELEVEN

"I'd guess we have about four seconds," Anakin said as he increased the ship's speed, heading toward the surface.

"You *guess*?"

Anakin cut back on the speed, almost throwing Obi-Wan to the floor. He leveled out the ship. "We'd better jump."

Anakin's calm was getting to Obi-Wan. "Excellent notion." *Considering that the ship is about to explode.*

Anakin raised the cockpit dome. They jumped to the top of their seats. Obi-Wan knew he had about two seconds to pick a place to land. Anakin had plotted the course well. They weren't over rocks, but a gradual slope. Still, landing would be tricky.

"Jump!" Anakin shouted as the siren began to sound.

They jumped. The Force pulsed around them. Obi-Wan looked down at the hard ground below. It became less than solid in his mind, an accumulation of particles and pebbles. It would yield to him. He would fall as lightly as a leaf.

He landed hard for the second time that day. Obi-Wan groaned. The Force was with him, yes, but the ground was still hard. He landed more like a tree trunk than a leaf. He fell onto his shoulder. He felt his tunic rip and a rock scrape his cheek.

Anakin landed more gracefully, seemingly without effort, and went into a roll to absorb the shock.

Above them, the ship exploded.

Now the danger was from the sheets of falling, flaming metal. Obi-Wan and Anakin kept rolling down the slope, gaining speed now. Obi-Wan saw a cluster of boulders ahead and simply rolled right up to it. Anakin did the same. They huddled in the shelter of the largest boulder, watching the metal fall to the surface and burn out.

Obi-Wan leaned against the boulder. "That was fun."

"Sorry, Master. I didn't realize."

"Not your fault. There was no way to know." Obi-Wan sighed. "Without transport, we've got a problem," he said. "We're in the middle of a wilderness infested with gundarks."

"We've got another problem," Anakin said. He pointed to the sky. A fleet of STAPs and two security transports with mounted laser cannons were headed toward them.

"No doubt the self-destruct sensor sends a signal back to the camp that an escape is in progress," Anakin said.

"No doubt," Obi-Wan said dryly. He scanned the area for cover. The only good cover lay in the deep craters. "Here's a question. Would you rather take your chances with a fleet of STAPs or a nest of gundarks?"

The first laser cannonfire thundered. Obi-Wan and Anakin exchanged a glance, then began to run. They would take their chances in the craters and hope to avoid the gundarks.

The cannonfire ripped the ground behind them as they ran. The air rolled into them with the shock of the blast. It was hard to stay on their feet as they dashed toward the deeper craters.

"Not that one!" Obi-Wan shouted as blaster cannonfire thundered past his ears. He recognized the prints of gundarks outside the crater.

Anakin veered. He was running fast, moving and weaving, but Obi-Wan picked up no communion with him, no Force connection. It was as though he were running with a stranger.

Anakin had lied to him. He knew that. Something had happened to him in that medical building. Did whatever it was somehow prevent Anakin from telling Obi-Wan about it? Or was it Anakin's decision to hide something from him?

I don't know the answer to that. And that means I don't trust him. Not completely. Not anymore.

One of the security transports dived toward him. Dual laser cannons blasted. Obi-Wan jumped, but the impact of the explosion against the rocks threw him further into the air. The next thing he knew he was falling, blasted headlong, deep into the black hole of a crater . . . and a gundark nest.

CHAPTER TWELVE

Obi-Wan landed on his sore shoulder inside the wall of the crater and ricocheted into midair again. He called on the Force to help him. He pictured a nest of gundarks at the end of his fall. He felt time slow down. He was able to pick out a clear landing site below.

He landed on a smooth stone floor and crashed up against a boulder, slamming his head. Relief coursed through him as well as pain. At least he had stopped in relative safety. There was no way to judge how big the crater was. He was more than a hundred meters into a pit left by an astroid thousands of years ago. He couldn't see through the black gloom. He could smell the gundarks, however, and hear them. They found the craters to be ideal nesting grounds, safe from other predators, and good bases from which to launch lethal attacks on their prey.

It was said that the cry of a gundark could freeze a being's blood. Obi-Wan didn't know about that, but the sound of them didn't make him feel very comfortable.

Gundarks had keen eyesight and good hearing. Their sense of smell was excellent. So far they had not realized an intruder was in their nest, but it was only a matter of time. He would have to use his cable launcher, and it would be a huge risk. The launcher would not reach high enough to get him completely out of danger. The sides of the crater were hundreds of meters high. Climbing out would be a long process, and would bring him into close proximity with the creatures.

He looked around cautiously. Through the gray gloom he could see now that tucked into the sides of the crater were deep caves. That was the source of the gundarks' noise. They were nesting there.

He peered above. He wondered how Anakin was doing with those security droids. Had he found shelter?

The roar of gundarks suddenly echoed in the crater. Obi-Wan began to quietly move away from the sound. He knew that if he was discovered, he could not fight the gundarks alone, even with his lightsaber and the Force. There would be too many of them. He would need Anakin.

He couldn't risk a glowrod. He felt his way forward cautiously. If he could find some footholds in the wall, he could climb it. Climbing would be slower, but it would attract less attention. He would have to risk the journey.

A roar and the sound of a gundark rolling over made him freeze. He could smell the creature. Surely the creature could smell him. Obi-Wan didn't move. He tried not to sweat. The gundark snorted, then rolled over again. Obi-Wan realized it was asleep.

He moved carefully away. The ground was more uneven here. Several centimeters of fine dust covered some kind of rock shale. It was slippery and the rocks shifted under his weight. When a rock slithered and cracked, he held his breath.

Nothing. The gundarks roared again, but their roars had covered up the sound of his movement. And the one in the cave to his left was still sleeping.

Obi-Wan felt the side of the crater at last. He ran his hand along it. It was pockmarked with holes. Good. He should be able to climb it without the launcher.

He put one foot in a cavity and tested it. Then he cautiously lifted himself up. So far, so good. He climbed up a few more meters.

He was balanced to take his next step when he felt a soft breath tickle his ear. Now he knew what it meant to have his blood freeze. He felt as though his veins were clogged with ice.

A baby gundark had snuggled into a deep cavity in the wall. It was sleeping only centimeters from him.

Just . . . don't . . . wake . . . it up. . . .

He could not have been faced with a worse prospect. It was disaster to fall into a nest of treacherous beasts. It was a catastrophe to blunder into one of their young.

Holding his breath, Obi-Wan began to ease his way past.

RRRRAAAAWWWWKKK!

The roar split the air. The crater shook with the impact of a gundark's running footsteps. The young gundark awoke. *Rrrraaaaawwww!*

Obi-Wan dropped the distance he'd traveled back to the floor. He ran. The gundark let out a scream and leaped up, heading straight to its young to ensure it was safe. Then it leaped down to deal with Obi-Wan.

The creature wasn't tall, but the strength of its four arms was immense. A common tactic was to grab prey by the claws of the massive arms that rose from the gundark's shoulders. Then the creature crushed the captured prey to death with the two slender arms that rose out of the muscled chest. The long, sharp claws could also rip a being to shreds. Of course, a gundark was also capable of simply tearing off the head of its prey with the large teeth that jutted out of its lower jaw. Once its bloodlust had been awakened, rare was the gundark that did not achieve its objective of rendering its victim into pieces of flesh and bone.

Obi-Wan was completely exposed, and he knew that caves were all around him. He couldn't hide. He drew his lightsaber even as he backed up but held it by his side, trying to show the creature he did not mean it harm.

But gundarks were not known to be reasonable.

The attack was ferocious. The gundark made for him, all four arms reaching, trying to claw him. Huge teeth snapped and saliva poured out. Obi-Wan smelled heat and anger. He was forced to slash at the gundark as it came at him relentlessly, its howl filling the cavity of the crater.

He heard the thump of footsteps. More gundarks were approaching. Obi-Wan fumbled for his cable launcher. He'd have to risk it. He sent it flying above. It hit something. He tested the line. He activated the launch, but the gundark grabbed him with one claw and threw him back down on the floor. He felt the jolt in every bone. He rolled away as the creature swung down to finish him off. The gundark missed, scoring the rock with deep grooves.

Four more gundarks thundered into the space, snarling, ready for the kill. Obi-Wan felt his back hit the wall of the crater. Desperately, he looked above. He reached out to the Force even as he sent up a shout he knew had little chance of being heard.

"Anakin! Anakin, I need you!"

CHAPTER THIRTEEN

If Anakin had felt that there was a veil between him and his surroundings before, he was now beginning to feel breaks in that veil. There were moments of clarity, brief flashes, in which he knew he was seeing reality. During those moments he felt something deep within him, like a hook lodged in his heart, and he was glad to slip behind the veil again.

It was odd that he was able to achieve battle-mind, but he had. The movements were so ingrained in him that he leaped and twisted and ran without feeling the effort, much as he did when the Force was with him. He had taken down at least five security droids on STAPs, and maneuvered so that another two fired at each other. He still had three more STAPs to contend with, as well as the Vanqor guards on swoops. He was fighting as well as he ever had.

When Obi-Wan had been blasted into the crater, Anakin hadn't had more than a second to react. He assumed that his Master could handle whatever was down there. Obi-Wan could get out by himself.

Somewhere inside, Anakin knew this was a curious decision for him to make, one that he wouldn't have made normally. But it seemed logical, too. Obi-Wan was a Jedi, used to getting out of tight spots.

Besides, Obi-Wan had always told him not to jump into things, to take his time. So why shouldn't he? His first priority was to take care of the droids and get the disk to Typha-Dor.

Anakin felt the veil slip again. It was happening more frequently now. He missed his calm. He wanted to be back in the garden. He didn't want to feel fear, or apprehension, or pain. He wanted to feel serene, as though nothing could touch him. He wanted it so badly.

Gundarks in the crater suddenly roared. Anakin fended off blaster rifle fire and drew closer to the crater. He thought he heard Obi-Wan calling him. The call came from within him, as though he heard it in his heart.

Something tugged at him. The hook that was buried so deep that he could barely feel it. He did not want to reach for it. He wanted it to lay buried.

Obi-Wan needed him.

But I needed him. And when he came, he asked for the disk. He did not come for me.

The pain this thought caused him to grab the remains of the veil. He wanted to wrap himself into its brand of unconsciousness.

I don't want to feel anymore!

Anakin leaped up and severed a droid in two that had the misfortune to pilot his STAP too close to the ground. Hunks of smoking metal clattered to the rocks below.

He realized what was wrong, what the essential conflict within him was. To be a Jedi was to follow his feelings. But if his feelings tortured him, what was he to do with them?

Grief.

Guilt.

Resentment.

Shame.

He had felt all of these things. Because of leaving his mother, because of Yaddle, because of Obi-Wan.

I don't want to feel!

He struck out savagely at a STAP that had come in low, its lone droid pilot firing dual blaster rifles. He cut the droid's head off.

"Anakin!" He could hear Obi-Wan clearly now, his voice strained and desperate.

I don't want to feel!

The hook in his heart seared him, and he knew its name. It was love.

The love he felt for his Master was lodged firmly within him. It was a connection that had grown from the first moment Obi-Wan had told him that he would take him and train him.

He had learned one thing about love: It was besides the point. It didn't make anything smoother, or better. Most of the time, it just complicated things.

Why would he want to feel again, when feeling hurt so much?

Why would he want to remember Shmi with guilt as well as pleasure?

Why would he want to revisit his torment over the death of Yaddle?

Why would he want to take up the burden of caring what Obi-Wan thought or felt about him?

Because it's right.

Anakin groaned aloud. The thing he couldn't get away from, the certainty within him, the essential truth he had learned through all his training at the Temple, that was what he could see now. He knew what was right.

He ripped the veil and felt the Force flood in with all its power. He realized that the Zone of Self-Containment had not allowed him to access the Force except at the most basic level, and he hadn't even known it. Now he felt it grow.

Along with the Force he felt his emotions again. They came at him in a rush, as if they'd been held back and now were free to overflow. They bombarded him as cruelly as the laser cannons shooting above. He wanted to sink to his knees from the tide washing over him, all the emotion he had suppressed and hoped never to feel again.

"Anakin!"

His Master's cry filled him.

He stood, drawing the fire of the droids and guards. He began to run. Explosives shattered the rocks behind him. Two droids on STAPs dived, shooting both blaster rifles at him, trying to catch him between them.

Accessing the Force, he tumbled through the gap between them, allowing the power of the blast to catapult him in the direction of his Master's voice, straight into the dark pit of the gundark nest.

CHAPTER FOURTEEN

One gundark had raked Obi-Wan's back with its claws. Another had thrown him against the wall. His left leg was going numb. He had killed one gundark, mortally wounded another . . . but would more come? He was weakening. He was losing. He was trapped in the dark with the roaring, ravenous beasts, and he had no doubt he would be torn limb from limb. They knew they had wounded him, and they were circling in for the kill.

If this was where he would become one with the Force, so be it. Yet he would fight to his last breath to prevent it. He would prefer a less gruesome end than this.

Obi-Wan thrust his lightsaber into a gundark's vulnerable neck. The blow made the gundark scream in agony and retreat. Obi-Wan whirled and retreated in turn as another bounded forward, its red eyes blazing with the scent of the kill.

Suddenly he felt the Force fill the cavernous space. A flash of light appeared overhead, and Obi-Wan heard a whistling noise. It was Anakin, leaping straight into the circle of gundarks, his lightsaber held in attack position.

When Obi-Wan had wondered if Anakin had abandoned him, he hadn't blamed him. He knew their mission demanded that Anakin get to Typha-Dor. But it had hurt him to think his Padawan could leave him.

How could he have held such a thought? Anakin would never have abandoned him. Anakin would never betray him.

Anakin landed on a gundark's back. He plunged his lightsaber into the soft tissue at its neck. As the gundark thrashed, Anakin leaped down and, twisting to avoid a descending claw, slashed at the next gundark, cutting off two of its arms.

Anakin had given Obi-Wan time to take a breath. He was hampered by his leg and shoulder, but he was able to join Anakin, forcing the gundarks back toward the deep cave that had formed under the curve of the crater wall. Anakin took the lead, fighting brilliantly, his lightsaber moving to deflect as well as attack, his footwork always pressing the gundarks back while protecting Obi-Wan from another assault.

From another cave, three gundarks tried to outflank the Jedi. Anakin sensed them moments before Obi-Wan. The Padawan somersaulted into them, taking them off guard. While Obi-Wan dodged to draw the attention of the first group, he watched Anakin spring up amid the second group. One gundark lost a leg, another its sight. A third recoiled as Anakin slashed at its chest.

The gundarks piled back into the cave, howling and screaming from their wounds.

"Thanks for coming!" Obi-Wan shouted over the noise.

"Any time."

There was a flash to Anakin's gaze that he knew well. His eyes were bright.

Something has changed, Obi-Wan thought. *Anakin is back.*

"They haven't given up," Obi-Wan said. "They're waiting." He indicated his leg. "I can't climb very well."

Anakin activated his cable launcher. "Then let's go the easy way."

"There are gundarks nesting in the cave walls."

"I saw them on my way down." Anakin wasn't troubled by the knowledge, that was clear. He grabbed Obi-Wan as if he weighed nothing and activated the cable.

They landed on a ledge that was free of a nest. Anakin activated the cable again.

"You planned the journey back as you came down," Obi-Wan said.

They landed again, and Anakin activated the other cable line. "Yes."

Obi-Wan marveled at that. It was what made Anakin a great Jedi. His battle mind was total and went everywhere. He saw every possibility, planned every move, and had even planned his escape.

They reached the surface and climbed over the lip of the crater. Obi-Wan took a deep breath, relieved to have left the horrifying nest.

He prepared to take cover when they emerged, but the sky was empty. He could see twisted metal and decimated droids scattered about.

"Did you get them all?"

"No, there were three STAPs left, plus two guards on swoops," Anakin said, tucking his cable launcher back into his belt. "I thought it was time to get you. I made it look as though a blast sent me into the crater. I imagine that when they saw me fall into the gundark nest, they thought I was done for."

"Most likely. No one survives a gundark nest." Obi-Wan looked around. "Now what? The only place to steal a transport is the camp. And I don't think breaking in will be as easy the next time." He looked over at the scattered remains of the exploded STAPs. "Can you make something out of those that will fly?"

Anakin surveyed the scraps of metal on the ground. "Are you serious? I couldn't even make a helmet out of it."

"How about fuel?"

"Possibly, but as you know, STAPs don't carry much."

"I left the swoop about twenty-five kilometers from here. We could refuel it."

"We won't get far," Anakin said. "I say we head back to the camp. Maybe I can figure out the departure code so we don't get blown up. How did you get into the camp, anyway?"

"You don't want to know." Obi-Wan groaned. He certainly wasn't eager to hook himself onto a flying transport again.

Obi-Wan's comlink signaled and, surprised, he answered it.

A familiar voice rang dryly in his ear. "Well, I'm here to rescue your sorry self once again. Honestly, I don't know what you'd do without me."

Obi-Wan grinned. "I think we found a ride," he told Anakin.

CHAPTER FIFTEEN

They had only minutes to wait until two red-and-white Jedi cruisers landed a few meters away. Siri was the first to appear, striding down the landing ramp, her short blond hair glinting in the sun. "Need a lift?"

"If you insist," Obi-Wan responded.

Obi-Wan and Siri had won their friendship through trials. They had always bantered and bickered. A deep respect lay underneath their light words, but it had taken some time for Anakin to see it.

Anakin was glad to see Siri, but seeing her meant he would have to see her Padawan, Ferus Olin. He wished that someone else — *anyone* else — had turned up to rescue them. The two of them had never gotten along, and things were worse between them since their mission on Andara, when Ferus had been abducted and

Anakin had withheld the knowledge from Obi-Wan. Anakin felt he'd had good reasons, but neither Obi-Wan or Ferus had understood them.

Ferus emerged from the starship. Tall and erect, he greeted Obi-Wan and Anakin with a proper nod. "Master Kenobi. Anakin."

"We're on another mission to the Xanlanner system," Siri said. "We got your distress signal. A couple of old friends of yours are ferrying me, Ferus, Ry-Gaul, and Tru Veld."

Anakin brightened. "Tru is here?" Tru Veld was his best friend. That would lighten the burden of seeing Ferus again.

He wondered if he would have felt this much pleasure if he had still been in the Zone of Self-Containment. He realized that the zone also blocked out feelings of intense happiness as well. He had paid a price for his serenity.

Obi-Wan suddenly moved toward the starship that Siri had emerged from. "I should have known!" he called. "That was such a wobbly landing!"

Anakin smiled. The landing had been perfect. But Obi-Wan was allowed to tease his oldest friend, Garen Muln. They had gone through Temple training together, just as Anakin and Tru had.

"You're one to talk about wobbling," Garen said, noting Obi-Wan's slight limp. There was concern underneath his words. "You look like you could use a medic."

"Maybe a touch of bacta," Obi-Wan admitted. "I tangled with a gundark or two."

"Ouch," Garen said. He laid a hand on Obi-Wan's shoulder. "Let's find the medpac."

Tru Veld bounded down the ramp of the other starship. His Master, Ry-Gaul, followed more slowly, his keen gray eyes surveying the landscape. Tru hurried up to Anakin, his silver eyes glinting. He was a Teevan, and had long, many-jointed arms and legs that caused him to walk like a rolling wave of water.

"Our paths cross, and it makes me glad," he said to Anakin.

"We're certainly glad to see you," Anakin said. "We have to get to Typha-Dor immediately."

Tru nodded. "That's why we're here."

"Who is that?" Anakin asked. He indicated a Jedi, a human woman with bright orange hair. She was compact and fit, and stood talking to Obi-Wan, Ry-Gaul, and Siri as Garen administered bacta to Obi-Wan's wound.

"That's Clee Rhara. She's an amazing pilot. She —"

"Once ran the pilot program for Jedi students," Anakin said. "She's a legend."

Clee Rhara walked over. "Anakin Skywalker. We meet

at last." Her shrewd eyes studied him. "I was a good friend of Qui-Gon's. We were students together."

"I'm honored to meet you, Master Rhara," Anakin said.

"No time for pleasantries. Better get aboard. I hear we have to get to Typha-Dor." Clee Rhara grinned. "It's going to take some fancy flying. The Vanqor ships are everywhere. Something must be up."

"Something is definitely up," Anakin said. "An invasion."

"Then there's no time to waste, is there?"

Clee Rhara turned and strode back to her cruiser. The other Jedi also hurried on board. Obi-Wan beckoned to Anakin to board with him on Garen Muln's ship. Anakin was disappointed to have to say good-bye to Tru. Not to mention ride with Ferus instead.

Garen settled into the pilot seat. With a glance at Obi-Wan, he tilted his head toward Anakin, and Obi-Wan nodded. Pleased, Anakin took his place in the copilot's seat. He felt honored. Garen was possibly the best Jedi pilot in the Order, as good as Clee Rhara.

Garen flipped on the comm unit to speak to Clee. "So, do we have a strategy? Those Vanqors aren't too keen on ships violating their airspace."

"Sure," Clee Rhara answered. "Go really, really fast."

The two cruisers rose and streaked into the upper atmosphere at top speed.

"Set course for Typha-Dor," Garen said.

Siri sat at the nav console. She entered the destination coordinates. Anakin kept his eye on the radar.

"Ships approaching," he said, giving the coordinates. "They look like patrols."

Four fast starfighters streaked across the sky.

"Piece of quinberry cake," Garen said.

Garen's hands were light on the controls. He climbed abruptly, the ship's nose straight up. Clee Rhara followed.

Garen headed straight for the two small red moons orbiting Vanqor. They orbited in tandem, and he dove for the space between them. He and Clee Rhara played hide-and-seek with the starfighters, who were unable to get a fix on their position.

"They're going to call for backup," Clee Rhara said. "I say it's time to outrun them."

"I'm right behind you. Let's go."

The two Jedi cruisers suddenly zoomed out from the protection of the moons' orbits. They streaked into the upper atmosphere. The Vanqor starfighters gave chase. Cannonfire boomed behind them, but they were able to outrun it. Garen and Clee Rhara maintained a zigzagging course, avoiding the occasional proton torpedo.

"We've got some kind of military ship ahead," Siri called. "Ten escort starfighters."

"Just a piece of juja-cake," Garen said.

"Three minutes until we can make the jump to hyperspace," Siri said.

Ahead of them, Clee Rhara dived as the enemy ship's huge weapons began to pound. Garen peeled off to the left. For the next three minutes, Anakin watched in awe as Garen slid the cruiser through, in, and around cannonfire without disturbing the gleaming red paint of his ship or even firing his own weapons.

Garen noted Anakin's interest. "I always prefer evasion to confrontation," he said with a grin.

The ship shot into hyperspace in a shower of stars. Everyone settled back.

"Typha-Dor in two hours," Siri said.

"Piece of sweet cake," Garen said, satisfied.

They came out of hyperspace beyond Typha-Dor's atmosphere. Anakin immediately checked the radar.

"No pursuit ships."

"I don't think Vanqor would risk violating Typha-Dor airspace," Obi-Wan said. "Not until the invasion, anyway."

"We'll be landing in a few minutes," Garen said.

Garen guided the ship to a graceful slot in a large

landing pad that lay at the space center midway between the two capital cities, Sarus-Dor and Ith-Dor. The Jedi were greeted by a security officer.

"May I ask your business —"

"We need to see the rulers of Typha-Dor immediately," Obi-Wan said. "We have vital information."

"The rulers of Typha-Dor are not easily seen —"

"We are Jedi envoys on a diplomatic mission from the Galactic Senate. We have information about an invasion," Obi-Wan rapped out impatiently.

"But . . . the invasion has already begun," the security officer said.

At first the officer refused to yield, but the combined insistence of eight Jedi was too much for him and his staff. The Jedi were ushered into the strategic planning meeting of the High Council at the space center.

The generals and the two rulers of Typha-Dor and their aides stood around a circular holomap. Blinking colored lights showed possible ship movements and attack points. Obi-Wan knew the two rulers as Talus, a young man, and Binalu, an older woman who had ruled Typha-Dor for many years. They had called for the Jedi originally and nodded politely at them.

"Sorry you were delayed," Binalu said graciously.

Binalu had stepped aside. Now Obi-Wan could see

Mezdec in the middle of the group. When he saw Obi-Wan and Anakin, he paled.

"This is a high-security meeting," he said. "You have no clearance."

"Mezdec, these are Jedi," Binalu said. "We asked the Senate for help."

Obi-Wan gave Mezdec a cool glance, then ignored him. He glanced at the strategy map. He saw that the Typha-Dor had massed all their weaponry and their fleet to the south.

He and Anakin had studied the invasion plans during the flight. Shalini had been right. Mezdec had given the generals false plans. They were massing troops and ships to meet an invasion that would not arrive. Meanwhile, the Vanqors would take over the capital cities in one thrust, unopposed.

"I have met Mezdec before. We were the team that was sent to rescue the crew at the outpost," Obi-Wan said. "Have you moved your ships to attack?" he asked the generals.

"We are moving them now," one of the generals said grudgingly, as though she saw no reason to tell the Jedi. "The Vanqors will attack our factories in the south."

"Is it too late to recall them?"

"Why should we?" the general answered. "With all due respect to the Jedi, we did ask for your help, and we are grateful for your response. But we can handle this. We are going to surprise the Vanqors when they invade our airspace."

"You, generals, will be the ones who will be surprised," Obi-Wan said.

"That is not the true invasion plan," Anakin said. He set Shalini's holofile spinning. It unfolded in pulses of light, showing detail after detail of the Vanqor invasion. "This is the real invasion plan. If you mass your forces there, the Vanqors will simply sail in and take over without a fight."

"But the Vanqors have already sent their ships," Binalu said, indicating the map.

"I see evidence of only two destroyers in the south," Obi-Wan said.

"Mezdec explained that more are coming. The crew intercepted the Vanqor invasion plans," a general said. She was tall and imposing, with multicolored medals on her shoulders. "He came to me personally. I am the high general of Typha-Dor, General Bycha."

"That's right," Mezdec said. "We have the plans. I was the only one to make it out alive."

"On the contrary," Obi-Wan said. "The others made it out, too. You'll be sorry to hear that, Mezdec."

"Mezdec is a spy, General Bycha," Anakin said. "I suggest you give an order for his immediate arrest."

The generals exchanged glances. Talus and Binalu looked at the Jedi.

"This is a grave charge," Talus said.

"They are lying!" Mezdec cried.

"You must trust us," Obi-Wan said. "The fate of your world lies in your hands. The Vanqors are not going to attack your factories. They are moving to attack the twin capital cities. Can you move the fleet to these positions?" He took a laser pointer from a general and indicated the map. "Look. The Vanqors are invading through this corridor. I've studied the star charts. Your moons will align to give them cover, but it will also create a window for you to attack. You can trap the majority of the fleet between the two moons. Even with a smaller force, you could defeat them. They will be vulnerable right here."

The generals looked at the map. They looked at each other.

"Don't listen to them!" Mezdec cried again. "They are lying!"

Slowly, General Bycha turned to him. "And what reason would the Jedi have for lying?" She held Mezdec's gaze. "I hereby issue an order for Mezdec's immediate arrest."

Then General Bycha turned back to the Jedi. "We don't have much time," she said.

CHAPTER SIXTEEN

Mezdec was taken away. The room exploded into activity. Obi-Wan was impressed with how quickly the generals grasped the situation and formulated a response. The fleet sped to the other side of Typha-Dor and lurked behind the string of moons, effectively concealing themselves and ready to attack.

General Bycha spoke to the Jedi. "We were unprepared for war. Our planet has no planetary defensive shield, and only one planetary turbolaser. It's all up to our fleet."

"You have the strategic advantage," Siri said.

"Which means there is another option," Obi-Wan pointed out. "Within seconds of the Vanqors invading your airspace, you will be able to surprise and surround them. They know their entire fleet can easily be destroyed. It is a perfect opportunity for you to force a surrender without losing lives."

General Bycha looked interested. "Most generals are primed to fight. I will do so if necessary. But on Typha-Dor we always seek to avoid conflict if we can."

"A truce would make sense for Vanqor as well as Typha-Dor," Obi-Wan pointed out. "Typha-Dor has vast resources. Vanqor has factories and technical innovations. The other planets in your system each have something unique to contribute. If there was a strong alliance between your planets, you would all be interdependent. You would learn and profit from one another."

"You could become one of the strongest systems in the galaxy and a boon to the Republic," Siri said.

Binalu shook her head. "But we don't trust the Vanqors. How could we, after what they have done?"

"Alliances are rarely built on trust," Clee Rhara said. "They are built on mutual advantage."

"One of your conditions would have to be complete disarmament," Garen said. "Vanqor might choose that rather than complete annihilation."

"It all depends on you," Obi-Wan said. "You have the advantage of surprise. When you don't fire on the Vanqors, they might hesitate to fire on you. You'll need to speak to the ruler of Vanqor and explain that you have his fleet surrounded. The Vanqor fleet captains will confirm. You have a chance to win a war without a battle."

Binalu and Talus gazed at the blinking lights on the holomap, each representing a ship with hundreds of lives aboard. They had a wordless communication with each other, then nodded.

"Tell the fleet to get into position but not to fire a shot unless ordered," Talus said.

"We will talk to Van-Ith, the ruler of Vanqor," Binalu said.

It was a tense time in the operations room. The generals, the Jedi, and the rulers watched the blinking lights on the map. They saw the Vanqor fleet approach. At the last possible moment, General Bycha gave the order for the Typha-Dor coalition forces to surround the Vanqor fleet. The movement was executed perfectly.

"Arrange for a comm transmission to the head of the fleet," General Bycha ordered.

While General Bycha spoke to the Vanqor captains, Binalu and Talus spoke to the Vanqor leader. The Jedi watched and waited. After a long negotiation, the Vanqors agreed to surrender and enter peace talks.

The Vanqor fleet slowly followed the Typha-Dor escorts to the surface of Typha-Dor, where they would remain for the duration of the talks.

"This will take some time to accomplish," Talus said to the Jedi. "Thank you for your help. We are in your debt."

"Shalini and her crew were responsible for obtaining the invasion plans," Obi-Wan told them. "They risked their lives. They entrusted the disk to us while they were interred in a prisoner-of-war camp."

"Are they in danger?" General Bycha asked.

"Anakin was also a prisoner," Obi-Wan said. "There's a camp in the Tomo Crater region on Vanqor."

General Bycha focused her intense gaze on Anakin. "We've heard of this camp. Rumors have reached us of medical experiments being performed on prisoners. This is against Republic law. If we knew this for certain, it would help us in negotiations with the Vanqors. Did you see anything like that?"

Obi-Wan saw Anakin hesitate. Why? What had happened to him? Why hadn't he told Obi-Wan? He'd had plenty of opportunity aboard Garen's ship.

"I underwent the procedure," Anakin said. "It is called the Zone of Self-Containment."

He saw the Jedi turn and look at him. Ferus's gaze was sharp. He had seen that Obi-Wan hadn't known this.

"What happens to you?" General Bycha asked.

"You become . . . content," Anakin said. "You have

complete mobility and your thought processes are sharp. It doesn't feel as though you're drugged. But the things that normally torment you don't bother you at all."

"Crowd control," General Bycha said. "It's a way to subdue populations. I can't believe we must form a partnership with those who would do this."

"The partnership will ensure that they won't," Clee Rhara said.

"How was the substance administered?" Obi-Wan asked.

"I don't know," Anakin said. "That was the strange thing. We weren't injected. And we ate with the med care workers and personnel, fed from a communal pot. Our water source was the same as theirs, too."

"It is possible they were all drugged," General Bycha said.

"I don't think so," Anakin said. "I felt that they were . . . envious of the prisoners."

"When did you first feel the effects?" Obi-Wan asked.

Anakin thought back. "They gave us a paralyzing drug, but that didn't make a difference to my mind. It was after a bath."

"It was transmitted through water," Obi-Wan said.

"That is a very difficult way to transmit a drug," General Bycha said. "Water transmission hasn't been perfected." He frowned. "These are dark days. There are too many scientists with no scruples, willing to poison bodies and minds."

Obi-Wan suddenly leaned forward toward Anakin. "Did you ever see the doctor in charge?"

"Yes," Anakin said. "I was brought to her because in the beginning I was able to resist the paralyzing drug somewhat, with the help of the Force."

"Do you know her name?"

Anakin thought back. "She never told me." Odd. He hadn't noticed that at the time.

"Do you remember what she looked like?"

"A woman in late mid-life," Anakin said. "Light-colored hair. Distinctive green eyes. She had a strong face." He thought back. "The strange thing was that she guessed that I was Force-sensitive. She seemed to know a great deal about the Force."

Obi-Wan closed his eyes. "Jenna Zan Arbor," he said.

Clee Rhara, Ry-Gaul, and Garen looked at him in surprise.

"She is on a prison planet," Clee Rhara said.

"So we thought," Obi-Wan said.

"Who is she, Master?" Anakin asked.

"Someone who has hurt the Jedi and the Republic in the past," Obi-Wan said. "She kept Qui-Gon prisoner in order to study the Force. She was a brilliant scientist who began her career after she found cures to several plagues and saved whole planets. But then she grew corrupt. She began to introduce plagues or viruses so that she would be hired to cure the populations. She was adept at using water systems or air systems. She made a great fortune. But the Jedi caught her in the end." Obi-Wan turned to General Bycha. "May I use your database?"

General Bycha showed him to the console. Obi-Wan did a quick check of the prison world he knew Zan Arbor had been exiled to.

He whirled around in his chair. "Escaped. She is now a wanted criminal." He stood. "We must get to the Tomo Crater Camp right away."

"You will meet resistance," General Bycha warned him. "The surrender is not complete."

Obi-Wan looked at Clee Rhara, Garen, Siri, and Ry-Gaul, a question in his eyes.

Ry-Gaul nodded. "We are at your service, Obi-Wan."

CHAPTER SEVENTEEN

After receiving clearance from the Senate for their operation, they flew to Vanqor. They met no resistance from the Vanqor ships. The Jedi cruiser flew over the rugged landscape of the Tomo Craters, and then the camp appeared ahead. Then resistance exploded in the form of laser-cannonfire. Apparently General Bycha had not underestimated the resistance they would meet on the ground.

Garen dived and twisted, piloting the ship expertly through the fire, never wavering from his destination.

They landed amid heavy fire and charged out, lightsabers at the ready. The security droids were taken care of with quick thrusts and backhanded swipes. The Vanqor guards were armed with blaster rifles, wrist rockets, and stun batons. The Jedi advanced as a solid flank that broke and re-formed as they leaped and twisted, using their lightsabers and occasionally Force-pushing a Vanqor guard who decided today was his day to seek glory. Instead he ended up with a throbbing skull as he was thrown against a wall.

It was at times such as these that Anakin felt something close to what he'd felt in the Zone of Self-Containment. It was not that he enjoyed battle. Battle was a necessity to an end. It was that battle filled his mind in a way that other things could not. Focus was absolute. He felt in the midst of the Force. With the other Jedi around him, the Force was especially powerful. It made every decision easy, every move fluid.

He even felt a kinship with Ferus. He did not want to be Ferus's friend, but he was glad to have him at his side during a battle. Ferus was known for his strength and agility. His moves were flawless. Yet he did not fight only for himself, but cast his battle mind like a net, ready to respond to the others if they needed him. When four sentry droids bore down on Anakin, it was Ferus who leaped, smashing two of them to the ground with one stroke.

Soon the droids had been reduced to scrap and the Vanqor guards decided that facing a squad of Jedi had not been in their job descriptions. They threw down their weapons and surrendered.

"Zan Arbor," Obi-Wan said to Anakin.

"We'll free the prisoners," Siri said. "You might meet more resistance there. Ferus, go with them."

The three Jedi raced to the medical building where Anakin had been held. No ships had taken off since they arrived. No doubt Zan Arbor had heard the battle. She could be hiding. Or she could decide to make a last stand. Anakin was prepared for anything.

The halls were empty. Doors were flung open, and there were signs of disarray in the trailing linens on the sleep couches and the discarded food on trays. The warming lights in the courtyard had been turned off, and the leaves looked shrunken and yellowed. It appeared that the entire operation had been hastily abandoned.

Anakin led the way to Zan Arbor's office. They did not need to break in. The door was wide open. Drawers hung open, empty. Her desk had been cleared. Even her septsilk curtains had been taken down.

Anakin felt relief move through him. But why? He wasn't sure. He only knew that he did not want to face Zan Arbor again. Especially not in front of his Master. It was as though she held a secret to a part of him he did not want to share.

When he turned, he saw that Ferus had seen his relief. Anakin hid his exasperation. No matter where he turned, Ferus was there, eager to see what Anakin wanted to conceal. Ferus's ability to tune in to his fellow Jedi might have been helpful in battle, but Anakin found it deeply annoying at other times.

"Too late," Anakin said to Obi-Wan. "She must have heard about the thwarted invasion."

"She couldn't have hidden all the evidence," Obi-Wan said. "We'll need to back up what happened here. It will add to her crimes."

Obi-Wan surveyed the hastily departed office. "I know one thing, Padawan. We have just discovered our next mission. We have to find Jenna Zan Arbor."

CHAPTER EIGHTEEN

The Jedi stood on the landing platform in the capital city of Sarus-Dor. The Typha-Dors had loaned a gleaming Gen-6 starship to Obi-Wan and Anakin, who were heading out on the trail of Zan Arbor. Garen and Clee Rhara had readied their transports to resume their interrupted mission.

Anakin leaned against the wall with Tru. He felt weariness deep in his bones, but he was anxious to get moving, eager to leave this mission behind as a memory.

If only he weren't heading to find Jenna Zan Arbor. Anakin wasn't afraid of the scientist, but he wasn't eager to tangle again with someone who could put him in the Zone of Self-Containment.

"It's got to be draining, no matter what the medic said," Tru said. "That's probably why."

Anakin smiled faintly. "Why what?" Tru had a habit of speaking his thoughts out loud, usually right in the middle of them.

"Why you look tired. The medic said he found no side effects, so I wouldn't worry about that." Tru peered at him sympathetically.

"I'm not worried," Anakin said. He paused. "Do you ever wonder about detachment, Tru?"

One of the reasons Tru was his friend was that he didn't have to explain things to him. "Of course. It is the hardest Jedi lesson," Tru said. "I wonder about it all the time. How can we follow our feelings and yet be detached? Master Ry-Gaul says that feeling deeply is necessary for all living beings. It is how we use those feelings that is crucial. If we let them determine our actions, we can go astray."

"I guess I still don't know how to free myself," Anakin said.

"Me neither. I guess that's why we're Padawans, and they're Masters," Tru said. "The thing is not to worry."

"Yes," Anakin said. "That's the thing." He noticed Ferus looking over at them. Ferus quickly looked away.

"What's the matter with Ferus?" Anakin asked.

Tru looked uncomfortable. "Nothing."

"Tell me. He's barely said a word to me. Not that I mind."

Tru shifted his weight. "He said . . . well. He wondered why you didn't tell your Master that you'd undergone that treatment. It was clear that you hadn't. We all wondered. After all, it is strange."

Anakin looked over at Ferus, who had joined Siri, who was saying good-bye to Obi-Wan. "He always gets in my business."

"He only said out loud what we all thought," Tru said with his usual honesty. "I bet Obi-Wan is thinking it, too."

"I'm not sure why I didn't tell him," Anakin said. "I was going to tell him. Did something ever happen to you that you wanted to think about first, before you told anyone?"

"No," Tru said. "I guess I like to talk."

Anakin laughed. Tru was always truthful. Anakin could see through him like water. That was how clear he was. And the only thing he saw was goodness.

Ferus came up. "It's time to board," he told Tru.

"I hear you're wondering why I didn't tell Obi-Wan about what happened at the prison camp," Anakin said in a challenging tone.

Ferus gazed at him. "Yes, I did wonder," he said. "But then I figured it out."

"Oh, really? Why don't you enlighten us?" Anakin suggested.

"You were afraid to tell Obi-Wan because you enjoyed it," he said. "You enjoyed feeling nothing. It even overcame your loyalty."

"Nothing overcomes Anakin's loyalty to his Master, Ferus," Tru said sharply. "And it is none of your business, anyway. You weren't there. You don't know what happened. You have no right to judge."

Ferus seemed to struggle against Tru's words for a moment. Then he inclined his head. "You're right, Tru, as always. I apologize, Anakin. I shouldn't have said it."

— *That's right, Ferus. You stepped over the line.* But maybe Anakin owed him one, after their mission on Andara.

"All right," Anakin said. He noted that Ferus hadn't said he was wrong. Just that he shouldn't have said it.

"Good-bye," Ferus said. "May the Force be with you."

Anakin merely nodded a cool farewell.

"Ferus is the perfect Padawan, remember?" Tru said as Ferus boarded the ship, trying to make Anakin feel better. "He feels like he has to correct all of us."

"Thank you for defending me," Anakin said. "I will miss you, friend."

"Take care, Anakin," Tru said. "Take *care*."

Tru walked away. Anakin felt a tiny sting at Tru's words. He hadn't meant them as an affectionate farewell. He'd meant them as a warning.

Obi-Wan waited as Garen and Siri walked up the ramp. It slid shut. Obi-Wan backed up a few steps to watch the two ships take off. Then he walked slowly to Anakin's side. They watched until the two ships were just red slivers in the sky, bits of light. Then they shot to maximum speed and disappeared.

"You said torment," Obi-Wan remarked, still looking at the sky.

"Excuse me?" Anakin pretended confusion, but he knew exactly what Obi-Wan was referring to.

"You said, *'The things that normally torment you don't bother you at all.'* Not the things that trouble you, but *torment* you." Obi-Wan turned to face him. "It was a strong word. What torments you, Anakin?"

He looked at the ground. "Perhaps I spoke more strongly than I meant to."

"That is not an answer."

"Sometimes I don't want to be the Chosen One," Anakin said. The words broke free. They felt like stones in his mouth.

"That's not surprising," Obi-Wan said. "Many gifts can be burdens."

"The Force is so strong. I can feel it so much. I *feel* so much. *I don't want to feel so much!*" Anakin hardly recognized his voice, choked and aching. Obi-Wan looked startled at his vehemence. "Why am I chosen? Why is it me? Can't I refuse it? Can't you let me refuse it? *Can't you take it away?*"

"Anakin —"

"Take it from me. Please, Master." Anakin wanted to fall to his knees. A deep tide of feeling, of dread, had risen up within him and choked him. He felt tears in the back of his throat. Even his friend Tru was afraid for him. Just as Ferus was. Just as his own Master was, the person who knew him the best.

What do they see that I cannot?

The sudden panic shocked him. It had sprung up so abruptly. He hadn't meant to say what he had said. He hadn't even known he had been feeling it. Now it felt like the truest thing he had ever said. The dread was always there. He lived with it, but he didn't understand it. He just wanted it to go away.

The depth of Obi-Wan's shock and compassion showed in his eyes, in the way he gently placed his hands on Anakin's shoulders. "My Padawan. I would do anything for you. I would bear your burdens for you if I could. But I cannot."

Anakin bowed his head. The panic and fear whirled inside him, and he was ashamed.

Obi-Wan bent closer to speak softly. He did not release his grip on Anakin's shoulders. "But I will help you. I will always help you. I will not leave you."

The words reverberated like a bell. Obi-Wan's touch brought Anakin back to himself. He raised his head.

"Things between us have not run smoothly lately," Obi-Wan said. "But you must never doubt my commitment to you."

"And mine to you," Anakin said.

The breeze rose and stirred their robes. It smelled fresh and clean. It was morning, and they had things to accomplish, a journey to make.

They turned, and together, they walked to the ship. Anakin looked ahead to the next mission, and the fear returned. Obi-Wan was bringing him straight to the creator of the process that had caused him so much doubt and panic. His fear suddenly freshened and sharpened. Now it was a certainty that this next mission would bring him too close to a truth he didn't want to face.

ABOUT THE AUTHOR

JUDE WATSON is the *New York Times* best-selling author of the Jedi Quest and Jedi Apprentice series, as well as the Star Wars Journals *Darth Maul, Queen Amidala,* and *Princess Leia: Captive to Evil.* She currently lives in the Pacific Northwest.

To

Jacob,

Merry Christmas!

Love,

Liz

2017

'Twas the night before Christmas,
when all through the house,
Not a creature was stirring,
not even a mouse;
Jacob's stocking was hung
by the chimney with care,
In hope that St. Nicholas
soon would be there.

Jacob was nestled all snug in his bed,
While visions of candy canes danced in his head.
And Mom in her kerchief, and Dad in his cap,
Had just settled down for a long winter's nap.

When out on the street
there arose such a clatter,
Jacob sprang from his bed
to see what was the matter.
Away to the window
Jacob flew like a flash,
Tore open the curtains,
threw open the latch.

Santa
please
stop here!
Love,
Jacob

The moon on the blanket
of new-fallen snow,
Shone bright as midday
on the objects below—

When, what to Jacob's
wondering eyes should appear,
But a miniature sleigh
and eight tiny reindeer.

With a little old driver,
so lively and quick,
Jacob knew in a moment
it must be St. Nick.
More rapid than eagles
his reindeer they came,
And he whistled, and shouted,
and called them by name:

To
Jacob

"Now, Dasher! Now, Dancer!
Now, Prancer and Vixen!
On, Comet! On, Cupid!
On, Donder and Blitzen!
Take me to Jacob's chimney; follow my call!
Now dash away, dash away, dash away all!"

And then, in a twinkling,
Jacob heard on the roof
The prancing and pawing
of each little hoof.

As Jacob pulled in his head
and was turning around,
Down the chimney
St. Nicholas came with a bound.

He was dressed all in fur,
from his head to his foot,
And his clothes were all tarnished
with ashes and soot.
A bundle of toys he had
flung on his back,
And he looked like a peddler
holding his pack.

To
Jacob

His eyes—how they twinkled!
His dimples—how merry!
His cheeks were like roses,
his nose like a cherry.
His droll little mouth
was drawn up like a bow,
And the beard on his chin was
as white as the snow.

Dear Santa,
I hope you enjoy
the sweet treats.
Love,
Jacob

P.S. The carrots
are for your
furry friends.

A big sack of toys
he held tight in his fist,
And he glanced to see Jacob
on top of his list.
He had a broad face
and a little round belly
That shook when he laughed,
like a bowl full of jelly.

Jacob

NICE LIST

Jacob
Steven
Glenn
Marcus
Lorenzo

He was chubby and plump,
a right jolly old elf,
And Jacob laughed when he saw him,
in spite of himself.

St. Nick winked an eye
and tilted his head
To let Jacob know
he had nothing to dread.

He spoke not a word,
but went straight to his work,
And filled Jacob's stocking,
then turned with a jerk.

Jacob

And tapping his finger at the side of his nose,
And giving a nod, up the chimney he rose.

He sprang to his sleigh, to his team gave a whistle,
And away they all flew like the down of a thistle.
But St. Nicholas exclaimed, as he drove out of sight—

Jacob, draw all your favorite
Christmas presents from Santa.

Adapted from the poem by Clement C. Moore
Illustrated by Lisa Alderson
Designed by Jane Gollner

Put Me In The Story is a
registered trademark of Sourcebooks, Inc.
All rights reserved.

Published by Put Me In The Story,
a publication of Sourcebooks, Inc.
P.O. Box 4410, Naperville, Illinois 60567-4410
(630) 536-1104
www.putmeinthestory.com

Date of Production: July 2019
Run Number: 5015191
Printed and bound in Italy (LG)
10 9 8 7 6 5 4 3 2 1

MIX
Paper from
responsible sources
FSC® C023419
www.fsc.org

Bestselling books starring your child!
www.putmeinthestory.com